Praise for
geography of an adultery

"The focus of Agnès Riva's compelling novel, *Geography of an Adultery*, is not on an affair but on the impact of place. Who we are is defined by where we are. Through the eyes of Ema, the reader feels the tension between passion and pulling back, between desire and the fear of being caught. Ultimately, the terrain explored is of a woman's needs, a couple's clandestine fantasies, and the shifting boundaries within relationships."

—Janet Skeslien Charles, author
of *The Paris Library*

"With precision and economy, Agnès Riva stirs up an uneasy and affecting novel that lives in the tension between constraint and abandon. As it depicts the quotidian, often ridiculous territory of an affair, *Geography of an Adultery* ingeniously maps one woman's inner world."

—Deborah Shapiro, author of *The Summer Demands* and *The Sun in Your Eyes*

"A powerful, gorgeous first novel."   —*Diacritik*

"[Riva's prose] borrows from the *nouveau roman* as well as forensic pathology...remarkable."   —*L'Obs*

geography of an adultery

geography of an adultery

AGNÈS RIVA

Translated from the French by John Cullen

OTHER PRESS
NEW YORK

Originally published in French as *Géographie d'un adultère*
in 2018 by Éditions Gallimard, Paris
Copyright © Éditions Gallimard, 2018
English translation copyright © Other Press, 2022

Production editor: Yvonne E. Cárdenas
Text designer: Jennifer Daddio
This book was set in Horley Old Style by
Alpha Design & Composition of Pittsfield, NH

1 3 5 7 9 10 8 6 4 2

Library of Congress Cataloging-in-Publication Data
Names: Riva, Agnès, author. | Cullen, John, 1942- translator.
Title: Geography of an adultery : a novel / Agnès Riva ;
translated from the French by John Cullen.
Other titles: Géographie d'un adultère. English
Description: New York : Other Press, [2022] | Originally
published in French as Géographie d'un adultère in 2018
by Éditions Gallimard, Paris.
Identifiers: LCCN 2021021299 (print) | LCCN 2021021300 (ebook) |
ISBN 9781590511107 (paperback) | ISBN 9781590511374 (ebook)
Subjects: LCSH: Adultery—Fiction. | LCGFT: Domestic fiction. | Novels.
Classification: LCC PQ2718.I86 G4613 2022 (print) |
LCC PQ2718.I86 (ebook) | DDC 843/.92—dc23
LC record available at https://lccn.loc.gov/2021021299
LC ebook record available at https://lccn.loc.gov/2021021300

To my grandmother Renée,
who expected so much of men.

geography of an adultery

the interior of paul's car

The interior of Paul's car is a space rather limited in volume and distributed with a certain stringency. The design of the four ergonomic seats is so precise that squeezing a fifth person into the back would be practically impossible. The front seats are separated by a short armrest half their height; it contains no storage console and provides no place to put such small objects as sunglasses or CDs.

With its leather seats, aluminum door sills, and stainless steel pedals, the vehicle's passenger compartment expresses its owner's intention: to possess a car that offers all available comfort and luxury, but in miniature, and for the price of an entry-level model.

Paul's smell pervades the space, assailing Ema every time she gets in the car. It's a very woody fragrance that mingles the man's usual cologne with his perspiration, though in more concentrated form.

After their separation, Paul will occasionally pull up next to her on the street, stop, and lower his window to say something. When he does so, inhaling that smell will suffice to unsteady the young woman for a moment, to give her the sensation of being sucked into that cockpit once again.

Almost from the start, Paul very clearly spelled out his view of their relationship. He invoked his shortage of time and his difficulties with personal availability, all owing to his family obligations. "We'll see each other at social gatherings, but face-to-face meetings, just the two of us—those won't happen very often." Having already had some experience in this sort of liaison, he also warned Ema about how painful it can be for one partner to try to envision the other's world, over which he or she has no sort of control. "Spare yourself. Don't make comparisons, don't compile a list of all the things we can't do. Otherwise, you'll run into a wall."

Ema made a show of understanding, although she secretly hoped she could cause Paul's thinking to evolve. She imagined being able to spend time with him far from home and their everyday lives, but since no getaway was currently feasible, she put up with brief encounters in restricted spaces, such as the interior of his car.

The car's internal trim reflects the man. The elegance of the decorative chrome elements, the leather steering wheel cover, the hand-brake handle, and the gearshift evoke Paul's sporty driving style. The maneuvers he makes are decisive but abrupt. No time is to be lost, no space to be wasted, and that's why he's chosen a compact, easy-to-drive car. Once she's settled in her seat, Ema always feels embarked, propelled forward, with no choice but to follow the motion.

———

There's something about Paul's sudden decisions (to make a detour before dropping her off, to commandeer her for a simple errand in a neighboring town) that Ema finds ravishing, as if the car has a magical power to transport her to an as-yet-indistinct elsewhere. At such times, Ema is overwhelmed by a feeling of confidence and absolute freedom.

"Suppose we take a trip somewhere, right now, just like that?" This is what Paul seems to be on the verge of suggesting whenever his car starts to pick up a bit of speed.

However, despite promising beginnings, these flights never lead anywhere, and sooner or later, the certainty of their pointlessness ends up depressing Ema. As for Paul, he doesn't seem to share her disappointment, contenting himself with the pleasure of rolling along in silence. Slightly irritated by what she considers his detachment, the young woman reacts by taking hold of the upper assist handle and trying to appear composed.

Paul is all the more at ease in his car because it serves as his second home. An expert in buildings and public works, he spends a great deal of time on the road, on business trips that have the added utility of allowing him to catch his breath.

If her lover knows she's home alone, he'll call her from his car, sometimes late in the afternoon, while driving from his swimming club to his residence. At such moments, the man sounds more relaxed than usual, having provisionally conquered an obstacle course or, more modestly, returned his focus to himself through his athletic exertions, as if he were never really available except when in motion, when leaving one point and on his way to another.

A perfect extension of his personality, the interior of his car is organized in such a way that everything is close at hand: his sunglasses, which he extracts from the glove box with a swift gesture, leaning slightly toward Ema; the seat belt comfort clip; the climate control, always running full-strength to maintain an indecently high temperature; the jacket he wears at work sites and keeps on the back seat; the safety boots in the trunk; and the short armrest, which allows his hand to pass easily back and forth between the gearshift and the young woman's knee, provoking discomfort in Ema, as if this automatic gesture shows that she too has been consigned to the domain of handy accessories.

It was to give Ema a ride home from the labor court where they both work that Paul first welcomed her into this very personal space of his. It allowed them to become acquainted.

One day, when Paul had stopped the car and a few moments of silence ensued, Ema seized the opportunity to declare her feelings to him. He'd just informed her that he'd lost his mother. It wasn't the first time she'd heard him speak affectionately about the brave, upright woman who raised him and his brothers and sisters on her own. Now, as Ema listened to his grief, it seemed to her that it was her own mother who had died yesterday. A barrier inside her gave way, and she felt a sudden urge to take Paul's hand and commune with him. They had been confiding in each other for weeks, but their relationship had not yet dared to speak its name. Ema was tired of her womanish procrastinating; she felt in herself the impatience of a man. She wanted Paul to talk to her about something else. She wanted him to talk to her about love.

"You need to know that I have feelings for you," she finally said. "And if you can't say the same, then

I think it would be preferable for us both to take a step back."

"It's a good thing you spoke first, because I feel it too, I feel the same attraction, and I didn't know how to admit it," Paul had replied.

Clearly quite disturbed, he had sat silently for a while before he spoke again, and a powerful sensation of vertigo had seized Ema; she felt like someone standing on the edge of a cliff, uncertain whether she's going to fall.

Since that first time, when she dared to put some words in a blank space, the inside of the automobile has become an environment favorable to intimate effusions.

The sound of the car doors closing them in brings their first relief, the satisfaction of finally being at some distance from the outside world. The atmosphere changes instantaneously, as if the banging of the doors were a signal.

Nevertheless, Paul doesn't drop his guard; he stays on the alert, inspecting the street and the pedestrians through the windows. "Our relationship must be absolutely clandestine," he often repeats to

Ema, his tone a little stern, perhaps briefly congratulating himself on the young woman's reasonableness, a character trait he's taken for granted ever since they first started seeing each other.

Most of the time, they park the car in town, not far from the labor court but always in an isolated spot. If they find they must settle for a place on the same street as the court, they're careful to pick one as far away as possible, beyond the traffic circle.

Once they've withdrawn into the shadows, they can observe the scene at a distance—the members of the court exchanging a few words before they disperse, the neighborhood emptying out as dusk comes down.

The positions they retreat to offer a different perspective on the social game and lessen a little the usual pressure to play it, especially as far as Ema's concerned, for as a general rule she's eager to get to gathering places, as if she were always afraid of missing an opportunity to connect with other people.

After they break up, this distance will be what the young woman misses most, what makes her fearful of having to experience events up close again.

———

The time constraints, the confined, narrow space inside the car, and their side-by-side (as opposed to face-to-face) position—all these factors encourage the couple to talk more freely. The car is the only place where Paul uses the word *we*.

Sometimes, when they've begun an important discussion and a meeting's about to start, they stay in the car, waiting until the last possible moment to spring out and rejoin the others. They speak to each other with such freedom that Paul is surprised and says so out loud. For example, on the day when Ema, blushing with emotion, made an effort to reveal to him the depth of the solitude in her that her marriage had not availed to fill.

"You're like an iceberg," Paul had said, teasing her. "The part of your personality that people can see is only what's above the surface. Underneath, you're a confused mass of affects and emotions that complicate your life."

This ease of intellectual exchange fosters Ema's fantasy of an ideal amorous space where everything can be said and understood, and it simultaneously awakens a physical desire that leaves her feeling unsatisfied when the time comes for them to part.

Because of the car's untinted windows and the ubiquitous streetlights whose bright halos illuminate its interior, Paul's and Ema's gestures remain constrained. They can allow themselves some discreet movements—they squeeze each other's hands in the darkness of the car, under the armrest, or Paul furtively strokes the back part of Ema's cheek—but embraces and kisses are not permitted until they're out of town. And even then, the man's attitude retains a certain stiffness; he has a way of casting off his seat belt expansively and then making an awkward three-quarters pivot toward the young woman.

The occurrence of these privileged moments is completely dependent on Paul's convenience, on whether he passes and picks her up or she's obliged to make the drive by herself, at the wheel of her own car, and whether he takes her straight home or decides to postpone for a little while the moment of their parting. Ema thus finds herself subordinate to the imperatives of his schedule.

As the weeks go by, Ema realizes that Paul is capable of going for days without showing her any sign of life. When such an absence grows too long for the young woman, who knows they can't speak freely on the telephone, the inside of the car allows her to reclaim him: "What's going on?" "Where were you?" "Can't you at least try to keep in touch?"

"Yes, you were worried, I understand," "I didn't notice the time passing," "I promise to pay more attention in the future," Paul answers at once.

Angry at first, Ema ends up murmuring to him, sweetly and affectionately, what she expects of him, namely that they will meet in a more intimate space, in a Paris restaurant, for example. But when no concrete response is forthcoming and the young woman starts to doubt, all Paul has to do is to seize her hand and look deep into her eyes and say sweet things to her, and they both instantly feel the spark again, and their attachment, the strength of their bond, appears obvious to Ema.

a corner in the kitchen in ema's house,
between the sink and the refrigerator

Because the young woman works only part-time, her
house soon proved to be a place for quick, discreet
morning visits until a better choice should present
itself.

Ever since her love affair with Paul began, Ema
has tried her best to reconcile her daily routine,
the equilibrium it's taken her years to build, with
their relationship, which unsettles and panics her.
Something in her has grown hard, and it helps her

to combat the elation that could make her lose her balance.

Often, when they're in Paul's car, her repressed desire to throw her arms around him clamps her chest so hard that she almost can't breathe. She begins to feel ashamed of that ardent desire, which gets no satisfaction. And then she wonders, *How can Paul control his passion so well?*

Perhaps because she has such a need for intimacy, the danger of provisionally opening her door to him didn't strike her as problematic right away, not even when Paul, weighing their possible rendezvous venues, took care to proclaim, in a tone that brooked no reply, "My home is a sanctuary."

"You really ought to put some blinds on that window," he says, every time Ema lets him in.

Ema's house dates from the 1980s. It's a starter house of a type to be found in every region of France, a basic model whose sole fanciful touch is its lavender blue shutters. From the man's first visit and the long embrace that followed just inside the closed door, to their separation, which will occur in the same spot, the couple's every impulse has been conditioned by the ground-floor window, because closing the shutters in the middle of the day would arouse suspicion.

This window and the roof window on the upper floor are the only two openings in the house that overlook the street. A transparent Dacron curtain, chosen so that its sheerness would let the light in, barely blurs what's going on inside.

As the street is fairly narrow, the intervening distances are small, and unless you're alert to the slightest sound, people's faces, framed by the window, appear all at once, before you have a chance to prepare yourself.

Little taps on the window often make Ema turn around to discover the mailman, his nose squashed against the glass, impatiently scanning the interior of the room for her so that he can deliver a piece of registered mail or a parcel.

She has also learned to distinguish the sound her husband's car makes when it turns onto their street, his rather clumsy way of shifting into reverse to park, grinding the gears, and the beep when his remote key locks the door. Shortly thereafter, her husband's silhouette appears more and more clearly in the window as he gets closer to the glass, through which he always takes a quick look, as if he wants to see something by surprise or make sure that everything's in order for his return home.

Before sitting at the living room table with Ema, Paul usually takes a little tour of the space, commenting on how the objects are arranged or noticing that a new piece of furniture has been acquired.

"That's exactly the shape and color I want when I get new chairs at home," he said one day, gesturing at a white polymer armchair with a curved design. "It'll be my seat when I come here, if that's all right with you," he allowed himself to add, laughing as he did so.

At first, his way of making himself at home surprised the young woman, but then she learned from Paul's own mouth that all his previous mistresses had been single or divorced, which explained his tendency to consider the places where his partners lived as extensions of his own. At bottom, his casual attitude doesn't bother Ema, who rather sees in it a jealous attempt on her lover's part to reassert his claim to her by joking a bit about the projects and purchases she's undertaken with another man.

Once they're sitting down with their cups of coffee, they talk about this and that, about their common

activities at the labor court or about more personal
subjects, such as Paul's adversarial relationship with
one of his twin daughters.

"I almost called you up for advice, but I thought
I should figure out what to do on my own, like a big
boy," Paul sometimes confesses. One day, for example, he found photographs of his daughter on Face-
book and wondered if they weren't too provocative.

On such occasions, Ema catches a glimpse of the
importance her opinions may have for him, and the
insight surprises her, given her lack of self-confidence.
In fact, Paul never misses a chance to lecture her on
this very subject, ever since they were in a court session together and he noticed she was prone to letting
her emotions get the best of her.

"You have to compartmentalize," he often tells
her. "Don't let your personal feelings affect judg-
ments that must remain rational."

When her lover talks like this, the impact that the
look in his eyes and his schoolmasterish tone have on
her is complex, being both aggravating and sexually
arousing. Paul's the first man in a long time who's
so familiar with her social activities and her personal
organization. She realizes how much she needs to get
some perspective on her work, to take a structured,

pragmatic approach, and how feverishly she waits for his approval. Is he even aware of the influence he has over her?

Every now and then, if he's overwhelmed with work, he may pull out his cell phone and his calendar and set about dealing with some business matters from her house so that he can stay in her company longer.

His mere presence, even if he's busy, soothes Ema; she suffers during his periods of absence, when not a word, not a text message arrives to calm her doubts, to dismiss the idea that he might be taking their relationship lightly.

When he has time to devote to her and his visits become more frequent, she gains confidence, and she likes to imagine that soon her house will stop being their refuge and become simply a place for them to meet and catch up on each other's news over coffee—just an interim location where they can spend a little time while awaiting an opportunity for their next "real encounter."

The urge to embrace invariably leads them to the recess in the kitchen; a distinctive feature of this nook is that it's screened from the ground-floor window by a glazed wall in a metal frame.

Ema's only concessions to modernity were to install roller shutters on all the bedroom windows and to give the kitchen an American-style renovation: black and white acrylic furniture and built-in appliances, the whole arranged in a U shape whose left side is prolonged by a serving table that extends to the middle of the living room.

Everywhere else, the house has remained as it was when it was purchased: a standard middle-class dwelling unit whose simplicity may ultimately give way to something extraordinary, something that Ema has always been convinced can come only from the outside.

The corner they retreat to is located between the sink and the refrigerator. On one side, along the back wall, a storage cabinet. On the other, the sink and a work counter. Above this space, a stretched fabric forms a decorative false ceiling, in which several recessed lights are set, and which leads to a bell-shaped metal oven hood. Behind the gas stove, a window with two sliding casements overlooks the garden and, on one side, the veranda of the house next door.

Narrow though it is, this space proves in the end to be better suited to quenching their thirst for physical union than the inside of Paul's car, where they move stiffly and clumsily.

Ema passionately abandons herself to Paul's kisses and caresses. The extremely thin and rather dry skin of his lips, which are two almost closed lines at first and then open wide on hers. The strange sensation, after her husband's balding pate and bare nape, to touch her lover's thicker, longer hair, the curls covering the back of his head. Then Ema's hand, undoing a few buttons and sliding under Paul's shirt to caress his hairless chest as she presses her body against his. The man's slow, delicate movements, his hands lightly stroking her breasts, her stomach, her face.

The innocent contact of this warm, supple body seems to refute the distance, a mixture of authority and reserve, that Paul usually maintains between them, a distance also connected to his greater experience in amorous relationships.

She wants Paul to be moved; she wants him to shed his carapace for a moment and abandon himself in her arms. So close to her, breath to breath, he reveals a timidity she takes as a good sign, as if the fact of getting undressed, if only partially, puts them on an equal plane, where they're both as ardent as if they were experiencing those emotions for the first time.

"I don't think we'll ever be more excited than this," Paul murmurs in Ema's ear after a long kiss, as if he wants her to take the next step but has no intention of forcing her.

The young woman categorically refuses to let herself be taken standing up, as if such crudeness were more than she could bear, or as if she'd rather not abet a sort of pillage on her marital territory, the idea of which, she suspects, arouses her lover.

And so they intentionally maintain their uncomfortable position, leaning on the edge of the counter, Ema always pressing her bottom against the side of the sink, turning her eyes in the direction of the downstairs window, her view of which is blocked by the glazed wall, and placing her whole body incongruously in respect to the ordinary functions of a kitchen, definitively turning her back on a space where she usually busies herself and bends to her work.

It sometimes happens, however, that the positions are reversed, as they were, for example, on the day when they'd had one of their first quarrels, and Paul, feeling responsible for it, implored her to join him in the corner: "Come to my arms, let me feel whole again." Then he braced his lower back against the sink, and it was Ema's turn to nestle against him. Her perspective was changed, and now she was gazing through the kitchen window at the garden she'd loved at first sight, with the fruit trees that gave it the look of an orchard and, in the summer, provided refreshing shade.

She's fallen into the habit of taking a stroll in the garden at the end of the day to think about Paul. At those moments, her desire for him gives her a feeling of omnipotence and abolishes distances. If he's just called, Ema sits on a patch of grass, phone in hand, and resumes the conversation with him. She's amazed at the power of words, which sometimes, at some point in one of their more passionate exchanges, manage to soothe her physical desire for him a little.

Otherwise, she goes all the way to the wooden fence, at the very end of the garden, and stays there awhile, her eyes turned toward the nearby town where her lover lives, until her neighbor waves to her, interrupting her meditations, or she hears her husband's car in the driveway.

Ema's house has always constituted a refuge for her, a place for regaining her strength, the first place she's really made her own. When she's in Paul's arms, when they're clasping each other close in their corner, she feels she's protected by a magic shield. Her perception of her house takes on a sort of unreal tinge at such moments, which makes moving about in it easier for her once he's gone.

The recent modernization of the kitchen helps her greatly in imagining herself elsewhere. The corner where she and Paul take cover, between the sink and the refrigerator, seems not to exist as such except when she's with him. The rest of the time, when she's with her family, the corner recedes, becomes part of a larger area, and even disappears completely, transformed into a simple corridor as people move from the fridge to the serving table, from the sink to the cupboard.

In spite of everything, when she and Paul finally succeed in detaching themselves from each other, Ema attempts to make him understand that this situation, these embraces in her family home, can't go on.

Before she states her case, Ema seeks to place herself as far away from her lover as she can, leaning against the glass door of the dining room with her hands behind her back. But when she starts to speak, only fragments of sentences and disconnected words come out, as if she were under a spell—like one of those fairy-tale princesses who open their mouths and cough up frogs or pieces of gold.

One day when Paul's not working, he comes to visit Ema early in the afternoon, and their erotic games go even farther than usual.

"That's enough," the young woman says, breaking away from her lover, balking at his taste for casual satisfaction. "If you want to make love, let's take your car and look for a hotel."

The hexagonal space they're occupying, which ordinarily facilitates their movements because of their vertical position and the precise way they must place themselves—like actors hitting their marks on a movie set—no longer seems to her like more than what it is: a narrow recess about one and a half meters square.

"I can't get away," Paul explains. "I took today off to do some work, and I'm expecting a delivery. I'm very sorry."

Once the man has left, Ema finds herself alone inside the walls of her house, all her energy gone.

When she and Paul part after they've met some-where outside, she's generally delighted to be carry-ing on a secret relationship. Even her house seems different: the walls protective, the space uncluttered and brighter than usual, the idea of their love so vivid that she could touch it; all she'd have to do is to reach out her hand.

But now that Paul has vacated the premises, leaving her in their disorder, the inside of her home seems morbidly luminous, like something perceived in a confused state where different times get jum-bled together and you don't know for sure which one you're in. She feels incapable of concentration, with-out enough strength to do anything more than take a bath and let the rest of the day float by.

That night she has a dream. Paul calls her up, and she goes to meet him in a room where he's alone, seated behind a desk. He starts giving her instruc-tions, incessantly sorting through files as he speaks.

"I've opened this folder for us," he explains be-nevolently, showing her how to access it on the com-puter. "You can put whatever you like in it."

Then he looks at his watch, says he has an appointment and must leave at once, and vanishes, leaving Ema feeling an intolerable void.

"Where did he go?" the young woman wonders in her dream. "Where can he be now?"

the chapel

Sometimes they make an escape in the evening, after the court meetings adjourn. Paul takes her to the edge of town, to a sort of no-man's-land consisting of a big, empty lot and, across the road, a monastery where some nuns live.

The façade of this edifice—a large, charmless stone-and-concrete building with a zinc roof—features little rectangular openings fitted with curved, spiked bars. More originality can be seen in the chapel, a small-scale, contemporary creation that abuts the main structure and takes the form of a flat-roofed concrete cube; its uncluttered lines indicate that it was a later addition, probably from the 1970s, and that it was most likely the work of an architect. The chapel's façade, which parallels a poplar hedge, is pierced by stained-glass windows in the shape of elongated rectangles. Inside, the narrow windows and the weak light they shed, the ivory color of the little tiles that form an indiscernible mosaic on the walls, the slender iron cross above the door, and the general sobriety of the whole produce an atmosphere favorable to quiet reflection.

The pediment of the chapel bears an inscription, "Icarus," whose meaning remains mysterious. Did the architect want to connect the building to the streets in the adjacent neighborhood, which are named after famous aviators, or is the inscription a warning to the sisters about the dangers of technological advances?

Out-of-the-way as it is, the chapel attracts fewer of the faithful than the churches in the surrounding town centers do. As for Paul, he attends Sunday services at a Protestant house of worship whose yellowish façade reminds Ema of the ready-to-paint Nativity figurines children are given at Christmas. The front of this church faces the town's main thoroughfare and is a landmark for local public figures, who always linger for a moment in the enormous square. Since the covered market is located only a few meters away, a short walk allows politicians to show themselves to their constituents during election season. For some time now, Paul has become more assiduous about going to church, accompanied by his family. Ema can't help feeling betrayed, as if his solidifying his family structure in this way can be accomplished only at her expense.

The young woman practices no religion, but she finds that the chapel's simplicity draws her inside. On the eve of her mother's funeral, shattered by the local priest's refusal to conduct the service on the pretext that Ema and her husband weren't known parishioners, she went and knocked on the nuns' door.

The sisters apologized for being unable to leave their religious house to go to the cemetery, but they promised to say prayers in Ema's mother's memory. Her mother found a place of welcome within those walls, as if it were an urgent necessity—because of her intolerable suffering—that a door open for her somewhere, anywhere at all. And on that day at the entrance to the convent, the sisters' round faces under their headdresses, as they leaned slightly forward, were filled with compassion.

When they park the car in front of the monastery, Paul usually traps Ema's hand—which she often places on his knee—in his own; then they stay that way for a long moment without saying anything, giving their emotions time to gather force again.

"I don't believe we have the same expectations," the young woman says to her lover, her voice trembling a little as she forces herself to meet his eyes. "It's clear to me that I'm more involved than you."

Her attempts to establish routines that can be counted on, like her offer of her house as a place where they can see each other outside of work, have ended in failure, for Paul's visits remain as irregular as always. Between one encounter and the next, it seems to her, the man quite simply forgets her; he

30

moves on to something else. The business matters that absorb him form an irreducible block of time into which he disappears.

Paul hesitates before answering her, as if thoroughly preparing what he's going to say. Often, what he says to the young woman is, "Figure me out," an allusion to his difficulties in making a commitment, and this formulation tends to irritate Ema, who thinks she detects in it the man's penchant for the casual.

"I have some very great expectations myself," Paul eventually says.

Then he sets about explaining that in the beginning, he was merely attracted to her, both by her appearance and by the intelligence he saw her demonstrate in the labor court, but that subsequently, ever since they've grown closer, his feelings for her have become more and more intense.

"We're going to have to manage our relationship much more delicately than I first thought," he concludes, speaking in a worried tone.

Next, in a way both a little blithe and exceedingly clumsy, he brings up his wife—who's less intelligent than Ema—and the ties that nonetheless still bind him to her.

Paul's remarks provoke the young woman. He has just spoiled their intimate moment, right when she was getting ready to give him Françoise Sagan's novel *Scars on the Soul*, which had thrilled her. She even hoped she and her lover could discuss it together.

There's obviously no way to extract ourselves from our daily routines, Ema thinks; the book stays in her bag.

The young woman takes a look outside the car. The minimalist setting is full of promise: the chapel with the sky above it, the silence that must reign inside it—these can't help bringing them closer together. It's a clear blue place in which, for once, they won't be bothered.

Ema has a very romantic idea of love affairs. In the thoroughly coded, circumscribed, and formatted world she lives in, a world filled with intrusive systems that threaten individual freedoms, it seems to her that amorous feelings remain an adventure exempt from all forms of control, the only truly unique and unpredictable adventure there is. She thinks that her faith in love is her version of spirituality. On that particular day, her conviction results in a sudden urge to see the inside of the monastery with Paul.

After presenting themselves at the reception desk, they follow a nun along a wide corridor paved with worn black and white tiles until they come to a dark vestibule that opens onto a rear courtyard, the doorway to the chapel, and a workshop where religious objects are made from olive wood.

The sister uses a remote control to open the chapel door and then returns to her post, leaving the couple alone. Inside the chapel, they're struck simultaneously by the silence and by a sensation of dampness.

As soon as they enter, Paul starts roaming around, hands behind his back, observing everything as if he were viewing a model apartment. His interest makes Ema wonder what significance visiting a place of worship might hold for him. The man has never liked accounting for himself, not to Ema, whom this quirk has already caused to suffer, nor even to his pastor, who reproached him the other day for not seeing that his daughters attend church services at school.

"I didn't even have a clue what he was talking about," Paul confessed to the young woman. "My wife's the one who usually handles that stuff. It was hard to explain to the pastor all the things I'm juggling already." Though Ema likes to imagine Paul taken by surprise, dissembling his irritation at being caught in a fault, this anecdote doesn't help her grasp what importance religion has for Paul, nor what's included in the set of "non-commercial" values he's told her he wants to inculcate in his children.

While Paul keeps his distance, the young woman stays on her feet, leaning against a pew, staring at the altar, as unmoving as when she was a little girl in church and would wait for the solemnity of the place to overcome her.

The cramped space of the chapel and its paneled ceiling make her think of a coaching inn. And, by extension, of an image altogether lacking in piety, a small hotel covered by an imitation thatch roof and located on the banks of the Marne river, a place of assignation—or so she's always been convinced—for licentious couples.

Then a memory comes back to her: her mother's friend the adulteress, and the efforts her mother had made to get this woman to go back home, practically against her will. The friend's husband, who looked like a priest with his bowl-cut hair. Not very sexy. Her mother's moral rigor. And then that Christmas mass her mother had made her go to in a dark period of her life as a single woman, when she hadn't stepped inside a church for years. The hard pew, the swelling voices. All her mother's attempts, back then, to prevent her from shutting herself up in solitude.

Why do my thoughts keep bringing me back to her? a surprised Ema wonders.

She glances in Paul's direction. He's standing still now, head down, hands crossed in front of his thighs, endeavoring to empty his face of expression and control his movements. But a slight twitching in his jaw muscle betrays his emotion. Ema thinks he looks like a penitent. Is he feeling remorse for having stupidly hurt her a little while ago by talking about his wife, or has he fallen into some other abyss?

The expression on Paul's face reminds her of something her lover said to her one day when she was confiding in him about the anxiety attacks she'd been suffering since their liaison began. "Each of us has a cross to bear," Paul told her. "Not being able to tell our spouses our troubles is our just punishment."

The young woman found these words astounding, coming from a man so quick to take liberties with morality. She couldn't resist scoffing at him, forgetting that he'd already gone through several painful separations in his life.

"You have no idea how conservative I really am, deep down," Paul told her one day, but the young woman persists in seeing him as she knows him, submissive to her wishes, capable of dropping everything on an impulse; however, she fails to consider that he might just be riven with contradictions.

The stained-glass windows shed a soft light, Ema thinks. Seen from the inside, they reveal themselves to be pieces of colored glass, crudely cut and set in some kind of mastic, like the polished glass pebbles she picked up on the beach as a child.

As she was exiting adolescence, she'd gone through an existential crisis. The idea of taking religious orders had titillated her a little as corresponding to her entire character, as the answer to her yearning for a commitment that would mobilize her completely. Then the imagination of everyday life in a community, of all meals taken together in some austere residence, had quickly dissuaded her.

One day, she'd asked her mother, "Do you really believe in God?"

"Sometimes when I'm with your father, when I'm in his arms, the emotions I feel are so strong that I think none of that can die," her mother had confided to her by way of response.

Ema had laughed nervously and made some ironic observations—to herself—about her mother's naïveté.

A little later, when they go through the main door and step outside, Paul says only, "Forgive me."

The panicky feeling she reads in her lover's eyes upsets the young woman and instantaneously dispels her dreams of union.

What's he apologizing for? Ema wonders, doubting that his request for absolution concerns only his earlier tactlessness.

Behind them, the loud click of the spring-loaded latch indicates that the iron door has closed, stranding them outside the chapel's protective womb and leaving them both a little bereft in the evening light.

the labor court

The labor court building combines a modern steel skeleton with glass and polished concrete panels placed alternately on its exterior walls. A marble plaque with the name of the institution engraved in gold letters adorns the main façade; the very traditional composition deliberately underlines the permanent nature of the court and its functions.

The building stands on an imposing paved square, extending in the back to the visitors' parking area, whose entrances and exits communicate in labyrinthine ways with the surrounding apartment complexes.

Inside, under a cathedral ceiling, the great hall is crossed by an ambulatory corridor with semicircular alcoves at intervals on either side. The curved seats inside the alcoves facilitate private conversations between attorneys and their clients or simple exchanges between people attached to the court.

On the periphery of the hall, narrower, darker corridors lead to the hearing rooms; the training and meeting rooms are on the upper floor.

Working in the same place as her lover brings Ema, if nothing else, at least the reassurance of seeing him regularly. But she worries about feeling needier and needier. For example, if Paul has a replacement fill in for him at a session, she can't help wondering why. *Where is he? Does he have some family obligation?* Her mind starts straying, prevents her from being completely herself, both in her role as counselor and in her dealings with other people.

———

When their relationship began, she told herself it was lucky that they worked in the same place. Their duties at the labor court opened up virgin territory for them, which they could develop without their respective spouses and which moreover responded to an important part of their personal aspirations.

The seat of the institution offered multiple opportunities for them to be together, whether before or after hearings, on their way to hearings, during training sessions, or while preparing cases. When they weren't in the company of their other colleagues, they liked to convene in one of the meeting rooms set aside for counselors, where they would often sit side by side and draft their reports.

The intellectual collusion that had united them from the start could be translated into concrete terms and applied to the performance of their mandate. Even though they come from different sectors of the court, their strong commitment and evident concord have led their colleagues to nickname them "the Associates."

This double recognition of them as a couple and, beyond that, as intellectual collaborators holds a great deal of importance for Ema. She would have considered it discreditable, not to say degrading, to be linked to a man only by mere adulterous games.

A discussion they'd participated in during those early days has remained particularly vivid in Ema's memory. Those present were colleagues from both sectors of the court—some representing employers, others employees—and they were all in the great hall, sitting on the curved seats under the cathedral ceiling.

Around them were the narrow, low-ceilinged corridors on the ground floor, their semidarkness contributing to a vague sensation of fear and perhaps to the idea that justice remains a mystery. Paul and Ema had just declared their feelings for each other a few days previously, and they were still reveling in the pleasure of hiding their secret from the others.

One of the members who represented employers had explained, in pedantic terms, that workers in our day shouldn't expect to get anything out of work, and especially not any personal satisfaction. From the determined insistence with which this person, who belonged to the same sector as Paul, continued to expatiate on his stupid idea, Ema thought she could tell that he was suffering. In a somewhat shaky voice, she

slipped in some reflections on her own way of looking at the subject; she pointed out how the "liberal"
system currently in place, with its emphasis on in-
creasing flexibility and employability, had forced all
employees to become detached from work and from
the satisfactions that it actually was capable of providing, and how it was imperative to rebel against the
offensive mounted by the free-marketeers.

From the opposite end of the half-circle ban-
quette, Paul had gazed at her attentively in his se-
rene, benevolent way, which contrasted with the
young woman's emotionalism. Then he'd cleared his
throat and spoken his mind with authority, denounc-
ing the ambient cynicism and the policies of man-
agement by terror, which sacrificed workers on the
altar of productivity. While he was speaking, a chord
resonated deep inside Ema, and she felt the surprise
of discovering how cruelly she'd missed that sort of
support and the astonishment of seeing that man,
sitting across from her, respond so perfectly to her
unlikely expectations.

Today, in the court building, Ema has a sensation of
suffocating. The place oppresses her; she feels more

and more like a prisoner here. She's tired, and she'd like to take her lover away with her to somewhere else, to some new, less constricted spaces.

Paul, by contrast, seems to feel more and more at his ease. He never fails to remind her how much the fact of having found a mistress as intelligent as she is to act at his side has transformed his life and made his work, he says, a real pleasure.

It humiliates and dismays Ema to see that he can continue to flourish in their work environment in spite of their lack of privacy and the attendant frustrations—until the memory of the panicked look on Paul's face in the chapel at last opens her eyes to what suits her lover best: places where their relationship can never deepen; places where he can, at his leisure, rendezvous after rendezvous, make his carapace a little thicker.

As their relationship stagnates, the tensions between the two lovers grow more acute. Ema sometimes forgets to be prudent, and on each occasion, Paul immediately reproaches her for her carelessness, addressing her as though she were a badly behaved child.

Late one afternoon, for example, after a session, Paul receives a phone call informing him that a friend's been taken to the hospital, and this news obliges him to leave the court at once. The young woman offers to accompany him to his car, which is parked in the visitors' lot. Once there, she feels so frustrated by his abrupt departure that she pulls him close to her and kisses him hard and long.

"I thought you were a reasonable person," says Paul, backing away a little.

Then, before getting into his car: "Since I'm not one either, we're going to have to be very careful."

When Paul drives off, she realizes that just behind the row of cars there's a thoroughfare from which any of their court colleagues could easily have seen them.

But it's not until the next day that she really feels the implications of her impulsive act, and she's greatly upset by the idea of the salacious comments that might be circulating about them. The shame of having let herself get carried away yields to a rush of indignation. *It's not my fault if Paul doesn't know how to manage a romantic relationship!* she exclaims to herself.

She understands her lover's need for security and control, but his perpetual reminders about limits enrage her. In the end, it's as if avoiding excesses concerns him more than experiencing what there is to experience with her.

Paul places himself outside of time, but Ema's keenly conscious of it. The more it passes, the more it threatens to trivialize the change that has occurred in their lives.

Once he told her, "Even if you left me, I'd still be your friend. And I'd hope that one day you'd change your mind." This declaration scared the young woman a little. She realized that not only would it be up to her to distance herself from Paul, but she'd also have to see about maintaining that distance, since he'd always be ready to resume, always be on the lookout, like one of those crocodiles that mimics a log and blends into the swampy landscape, lulling the vigilance of its prey by an interminable immobility.

Ema pictures their meeting—and the craziness it's brought into their lives—as a circular movement, a kind of cyclone with a central eye that urges her to keep on going, to seize this chance and not let it slip away, to live her desire to its fullest.

In principle, Paul wouldn't be against finding a place, an apartment, for example, that they could rent for their romantic encounters. But when they envision the passion they will know in their proposed love nest, what each sees differs a little from the other's version. Paul pictures a place where desire can be "contained," shielded from prying eyes for as long as their romance lasts, whereas Ema, by contrast, hopes it will allow their sensibilities a new freedom of expression. Such a place could give their relationship a truth it does not yet possess.

In any case, even though the man talks about renting a place somewhere, he never makes any move in that direction. Ema attributes her lover's indecision to his cavalier attitude. She still fails to gauge the degree of Paul's emotional disarray, torn as he is between contradictory forces that end up paralyzing him.

The celebrations planned for the centenary anniversary of the labor court further complicate the two lovers' lives, reducing a little more the space available to them.

For several weeks, lawyers and members of the court take part in the preparations, hold multiple meetings, and make any private moment impossible. The tension between the two lovers continues to mount.

The centenary celebrations finally come to a close one evening with a large gathering held on the court building's imposing square. Dozens of people are present, standing around tables under pole tents, eating and drinking. The attendees include Paul's wife and Ema's husband and son. This day also marks the end of Paul's term at the court, and since his profession is requiring more and more of his time, he's hesitant to run again. The young woman finds the idea that their collaboration's almost over—without her knowing what may replace it—simply unacceptable. And even worse, she and Paul are going to spend their last moments at the court in the presence of their respective families.

A reporter on hand to cover the event and take a few snapshots has the idea of putting Paul and Ema together in the foreground of a picture to show, for once, representatives of both sectors, employees and employers. The lovers position themselves on either side of the court building's main entrance, in perfect symmetry, and the reporter presses his shutter button. *At least our value to this institution is getting equal recognition*, the young woman thinks resentfully.

Ever since the beginning of the evening, Paul has been fluttering around like a butterfly, shaking hands, addressing Ema only to ask logistical questions, including the most boorish of all, tossed at her without shame: "Wasn't anyone in charge of providing garbage bags?"

Should the young woman try to speak to him in a more personal manner, his rather tense smile seems to say, *Let's not look like we're too close.*

Be careful, Ema murmurs to herself. *Always be careful.*

As her feelings for her lover grow, Ema's need for the two of them to be recognized by other people as a couple increases proportionately. She'd like to be permanently enveloped by his presence. As far as she can tell, her lover doesn't share the same desire. The outrageous distance he's keeping from her today makes her feel misunderstood and rejected.

However, her colleagues, busy all around her serving sandwiches and drinks, suspect nothing of her distress, which she's doing her best to conceal. Because their spouses are present, Ema can't allow herself to go to Paul and tell him what's weighing on her mind, and her anger begins to grow. It's not possible that a man as intelligent as he is can fail to perceive her dilemma.

In a photograph that the local newspaper publishes the next day, Ema finds an opportunity to assess the expression of her suffering. She sees herself staring at the lens with a broad smile on her face, her mouth half-open, practically laughing, even euphoric, but her body language is having none of it. Her tapered trousers, her tight sweater, and the purse strap slung between her breasts make her cut a dynamic figure, slimmer of late, partly because she's so tired. With her right hand, she reaches across her stomach to clasp her left arm, and the gesture looks like a protective move-ment, or like an attempt to hold something back.

After the photo session, Paul continues to amble about at his ease, wearing an untucked flannel shirt over jeans and an unbuttoned jacket, a little too big for him, that does nothing to hide his recent weight loss. Ema regrets that the difference between him and her husband—whom she sometimes calls "my skinny cat," amusing herself by pointing out something odd about him, by drawing a dividing line between the two men—now seems to be fading away.

When Paul's talking with people, he keeps his upper arms close to his body and spreads his open hands wide, but she senses in that expansiveness a false relaxation, dissimulating the desire to grab hold of something.

Ema notices that he lingers longest with certain eminent members of the court and wonders, for the first time, whether his great commitment, which she has considered altruistic, isn't a cover for more careerist ambitions.

This evening's success must be giving him some ideas, she thinks. *He's already calculating how to exploit it.* And she begins to suspect him of seeking out future allies for a project he probably won't consult her about.

This thought staggers her and opens the door to all sorts of doubts. Perhaps her lover has been using her from the start, capitalizing on their closeness to serve his ambition. In this kind of situation, are women always the losers? Is romantic dependence a weapon employed by men, even unconsciously, to keep their partners under control? She doesn't know.

Not far away, Ema notices a single woman serving fruit juice to children and already filled, it seems, with admiration for Paul's charisma. On this evening, Ema feels certain her lover is going to leave her, and she convinces herself that the juice lady will be his next mistress.

Now the crowd has split into two large groups, and the evening light falls on either side of the façade, with its tall tinted-glass door. Seen through this door, the interior of the building lies in shadow.

Several children are sitting together on the ground, leaning against a wall. Among them, the silhouette of Ema's son, his back rounded, his body cut in half, his eyes fixed on his mother, as if he guessed something.

A little farther on, the two lovers' spouses have come together and started chatting. Paul, an eyewitness to this scene, immediately steps closer to Ema and alerts her with a look. On the one occasion when she spoke to his wife, Paul told Ema, gratefully, "You

managed that well," and she found a foolish satisfaction in being complimented on her skill in the art
of deception. But this evening, for once, instead of a
man who "manages" things well, she has a hankering
for a man driven as she is by urgency, a man who
turns over the table.

Why doesn't he do something? Why doesn't he
ever arrange an evening for the two of them? How
can she bear the humiliation of being the only one to
want more, the only one to beg for a little intimacy?

Paul looks worried when he sees his mistress
coming toward the group he's in. She's shaking a little, nervously tucking her hair behind one ear. And
just for an instant, right there in front of everybody,
Ema feels a pressing urge to keep heading straight
for him, to walk into his arms, and by doing so, as
a punishment for his immobility, to blow up all the
barriers they've worked so hard to erect since the beginning of their affair.

the interior of paul's car, alongside ema's
house, as they're saying their farewells

"I was all the happier to go fluttering around left and
right because the fact that you were just a few meters
away thrilled me," says Paul, justifying himself the
next day, apologizing for not having noticed the turmoil she was in, for having been sure that she, like
him, was enjoying the success of the festivities.

The young woman remembers a lecture he
treated her to one day after listening to a pretty
pointed exchange between her and a member of the

employers' sector of the labor court. "You don't protect yourself enough, little lamb, you play your hand
too openly. All you're doing is offering yourself up as
a sacrifice to dishonest people."

In retrospect, that remark troubles Ema. Doesn't
Paul exploit her integrity too? Is he being sincere
with her, or is he just putting up a smoke screen of
words? Don't her romantic ideas make her particularly vulnerable?

Such doubts add to her state of confusion. In the
end, she persuades herself that the only way to make
her relationship with her lover evolve is to force him
out of his comfort zone, even if that means venturing
into spaces they've both agreed are off limits.

The first occasion presents itself a few days later,
when Paul gives her a ride home after a hearing.

When her lover drives her home, he usually takes
the precaution of stopping a little distance from her
house, along the sidewalk that borders the main
road. On such evenings, they always talk for a moment in the car with the engine running, exchanging

confused words, muddled by the imminence of their farewells and by the fear that some acquaintance from the neighborhood will catch them engaging in suspicious parking.

"I'll call you tomorrow." Paul often says this to Ema instead of "Good-bye," unable to project himself so soon into their next rendezvous. For Ema, it's a bit like being asked to "please hold" when the person she wants to talk to is on another line.

But the people in one of the houses in the development must be having a party, a rare occurrence on a weeknight, and cars are parked up and down the main road, so Paul is obliged for the first time to stop on the corner, just before Ema's street.

From where they are, the young woman can see the west side of her house. A big light-gray roughcast wall, and in the middle of it a simple honeysuckle plant, climbing up a trellis. Her house has neighbors on both sides and is separated from them by two lilac hedges.

The interior of Ema's house is more spacious and practical than it appears from the outside. To appreciate its true dimensions, you have to walk through the house until you reach the back garden with its many trees, overlooked by the windows of the two bedrooms, the frosted glass window of the bathroom, the sliding door in the kitchen, and the glazed door in the dining room.

The wall Ema can see from Paul's car is the garage wall; as for the front door, it remains out of her field of vision, hidden in a recess. Above it, the upper floor and a small room that serves a double function as a laundry room and a gym.

In the spring, the lilac hedges expand on both sides of the house and spread so far along the lower part that they hide a section of the front door. Then only the roof window seems to float above them, allowing Paul to know, according to whether that window is shut or tilted out, when the young woman has returned from a weekend trip or a holiday.

With her eyes turned toward her house, Ema tries to picture what's going on in there, to imagine her husband and their son. Her attempt, however, is not successful. Slightly tipsy, she's concentrating so hard on the idea of throwing Paul off balance that her mind glides over the image of the roughcast wall, blocks out the danger, makes her home and her lover's car two quite distinct, irreconcilable entities.

The feelings provoked in Paul by the sight of Ema's house are very different, as he's tormented by imagined scenes of her married life, including its sexual aspects.

This weakness on her lover's part gives her hope that their proximity to her house, to which he's about to release her, along with the pain of their imminent separation, will strike him with enough force to intensify their discussions, incite him to let himself go completely, and maybe even prompt him to murmur the words lovers use when they take off all their clothes.

Like the simple question—"So now what are we going to do, follow this inclination or not?"— that Paul asked her in a deep, tortured voice after they'd declared their feelings to each other. The entreaty that question seemed to contain—and most of all, what it suggested—rattled Ema completely and caused her to assess her inexperience with clandestine relationships and the winding path she'd have to take from that point on. Since then, she's tried in vain to vibrate with that same intensity, dreaming that those moments of emotion she'd felt in the beginning could be repeated forever.

Since their time is short, the young woman resolves to guide the conversation into the sexual realm without further ado. She describes to Paul her husband's angry reaction when she rather abruptly evaded his caresses not long ago.

"Couldn't you limit your intimate relations with him?" Paul asks her, lowering his voice, a little ashamed of himself for disregarding his own Rule Number One: *For nothing to be found out, everything must go on as before.*

But once his suggestion has been offered, Paul's mind is already elsewhere; his hand on the gearshift, his body tense, his smile somewhat frozen, he's no doubt ready to turn his cell phone back on—having complied with her request to turn it off—so that he can check his messages before he goes home.

Ema's in despair. *This relationship can make no sense and no progress,* she thinks, and she sees herself condemned, like the protagonist in *Groundhog Day*, to being picked up and then dropped back off indefinitely in the exact same place, where the man expects to find her again soon.

Although up to now she's acted with caution and stayed away from Paul's place of residence, this evening, as she once again watches her lover drive off, she thinks she has no other choice but to go there and put him in danger on his own ground.

paul's house

Paul's house, like Ema's, is situated in a housing development, but in a neighboring *commune*, or administrative district, and was built some years earlier. The young woman has seen the place before, but she's never been inside.

The residential area where Paul lives dates to the end of the 1970s, when dwellings were constructed on the site of a bankrupt industrial plant that used to employ a great many people. Still today, a mention of that plant awakens in the town's inhabitants nostalgia for days gone by as well as a persistent acrimony toward the current occupants. In the section where Paul lives, the houses are swankier than the ones in Ema's neighborhood. What makes the difference? Practically nothing: a mezzanine, a cathedral ceiling, maybe an extra bedroom.

Paul's house is a two-story building with a garage that has lost its original function and now serves as a storeroom. The man's car, therefore, stays outside, on a strip of driveway covered by an awning attached to the right side of the house and protruding beyond the front. The black spot made by the nose of the vehicle, seen from a distance, reveals to Ema that her lover's at home. When the carport's empty, the house becomes a hollow construction, a sexless zone, a forsaken territory with nothing to keep her there any longer, but sometimes the very bareness of the driveway, if she doesn't know where Paul is, evokes an image of abandonment that repeats itself like an echo in Ema's head.

The front door is located on the left of the façade, whose coating is light beige. A single large window on the house's right-hand side, rectangular in shape and featuring a stained-glass panel, gives to the whole an artistic touch lacking in Ema's residence, with its plain gray roughcast walls. However, the absence of the big picture windows found in more recent, more upscale homes places this one in the mid-market range.

The very steep main roof forms an overhang that rests on three columns. This roof is pierced by one window and two skylights—the twins' bedrooms— as well as a somewhat unusual air vent, small and pyramidal in shape, that looks like a surveillance periscope.

The three windows on the second floor are identical. Right below them are the front steps and a door with a heavy handle, and in front, at the end of a little walkway between two square patches of grass, the luxury of an individual green metal mailbox, perched on a post.

The exterior of Paul's house offers little insight into the man's private life. Every opening in the façade has an off-white veil drawn across it, one of those thick fabrics that don't completely hide what's inside but make furniture and people impossible to discern.

The rare details that provide a glimpse of her lover's family life are irresistibly attractive to Ema, but at the same time, and to an equal degree, they make her uneasy. The roof windows in his daughters' bedrooms, for example, are often open during the day, revealing part of a bedsheet or a *boutis*, a Provençal quilt, hanging outside. The colors of the *boutis* take the young woman back to her childhood, evoking the memory of a baby carriage and the little quilt she used to cover her doll.

On the side of the house, if you lean over a remote-controlled sliding gate, it's also possible to get a peek at a sliver of the couple's rather neglected garden and the lawn that Paul eventually will have paved over.

Green plastic fence slats and a basketball hoop rise above the garden wall, and a few bricks are also visible, part of a permanent barbecue built for Sunday afternoons spent with their neighbors from across the way. Paul loves to boast about this friendship to Ema, and also about how efficiently he and his neighbor have organized things, how they take turns watching each other's house when one of them is away on vacation, how they do odd jobs together. Part of his notorious daily routine, filled with obligations, which he makes immoderate use of to cancel appointments with her at the last minute; it's as though the man has invented all these things to keep her at a distance.

Ever since the twins started junior high school, it's become riskier and riskier for Ema to venture close to the house during the day. Their schedules are irregular, and their comings and goings must have multiplied.

When it happens that Ema approaches the house to put some work documents in the mailbox, the place seems to be immersed in ghostly silence. At such times, the house appears to slip into the background, to hide its blemishes and its defects, the better to highlight how incongruous it is that the young woman is in the vicinity.

On other occasions, the house shows its hostility openly; for example, when the incredible brush seal on the mailbox resists her efforts to thrust documents into it.

Like any person preparing to penetrate for the first time into a place she's been awfully curious about, the young woman is very excited by the idea of ringing the doorbell out of the blue. She hopes she finds Paul home alone.

Her main intention is to shake up the man and force him to change, but she's also eager to capture a snapshot of a life that goes on without her, in order to get better acquainted with her own desire.

A few seconds after Ema rings the bell, Paul comes to open the door, his face showing the resolve of a man ready to discourage a canvasser. His body is outlined in the doorway, while a background noise behind him, perhaps a vacuum cleaner, indicates the presence of another person.

The man's unshaven for a change, and he's wearing a raggedy T-shirt and jeans with holes in them—clothes for lounging around the house.

"Well, come on in," he says, opening the door wide, heartily inviting Ema inside, and immediately neutralizing her determination to knock down every barrier.

His reaction surprises the young woman, who doesn't realize, at least not right away, that Paul's desire for control causes him to be always one step ahead of her. It's as if he'd rather lower his guard in this situation than protect himself and risk losing the match.

In contrast to Ema's house, Paul's has an entrance hall in which half the space is taken up by a large, straight metal staircase; a large mirror on the back wall reflects the man's silhouette, reinforcing the image of a narrow passage, a checkpoint where you have to show your credentials.

The ground floor comprises a living/dining room and an adjoining room whose door is located beside the mirror, and it's from that room that the sounds of the cleaning lady at work can be heard.

The room, initially used as an office with a computer station, has forever been the subject of discussions between Paul and his wife, who wants to transform it into an art studio where she can paint. Paul's having a hard time resolving this issue. One day, speaking of the room, he'll say to his mistress,

"Why not keep it for our rendezvous?"—a pretty weak but nonetheless revelatory joke, as if the need for a space of their own titillates him too, though he can't bring himself to undertake any concrete steps in this regard.

The living/dining room downstairs is L-shaped, running the whole length of the house and extended on the left-hand side by a fitted kitchen, which is separated from the rest of the room by a low wall strewn with kitchen utensils and the twins' mouse cage. The rear windows of the house overlook a small yard. It contains a cedar tree, pollarded to limit its exposure to wind, and one can spot, relegated to a corner, the exhaust vent of an old air-conditioning unit.

On the second floor, a landing gives access to the parental suite and to a mezzanine that the girls use as a relaxation area, with video game consoles and board games. The girls' bedrooms and an attic are on the third floor.

The living/dining room, the heart of the man's household, has the look of an empty stage. Less vast than Ema imagined, it's cluttered with kitchen accessories (cooker hood, induction plates) half out of their boxes. Contemporary paintings—abstract geometric forms in shades of red, perhaps chosen for their color, which harmonizes with the colors of the sofa and the leather armchairs—hang above a modern fireplace. The steel of the cooker hood answers the aluminum fireplace surround. There's nothing warm about the room, though, and the effect of the whole is an impression of something frozen and rigid, like a paralyzed limb that can't be used anymore.

Ema reads Paul's absences into what she sees; some of his business trips can require him to spend several consecutive days out of town.

So if the man eludes her, it's not because of his home life, to which he supposedly devotes all his time.

All things considered, the inside of Paul's house is little different from Ema's. But then again, what was the young woman expecting? A cathedral ceiling, maybe, light wells like those in houses designed by architects, one of those surprising arrangements, glimpsed elsewhere, that might seem unlikely here, given the house's exterior dimensions, but that she thought she'd find here all the same. The principal difference is the extra room, the one the man's taking so long to decide what to do with.

After their separation, Paul will sometimes allude ironically to divorced persons they both know and declare, repeatedly, "We would have gone to live in Seine-et-Marne," as if the fact of moving to an alternative *département* a few kilometers away, as their friends did, would authorize every fantasy.

The man invites her to sit at the living room table, where he's spread out what look like construction plans for a building. There's also a cup of coffee, still steaming, and an empty mug. This mug left on the table suggests to Ema that, at least in the mornings, Paul's wife takes the opportunity to spend a calm moment with him, reading or working at his side, before she leaves.

"If it were possible for us to live together, life would be rosier," the man declared one day. Ema, however, told herself that even if they should decide to free themselves from their familial bonds, Paul's race against time, the permanent state of flight he was in, would remain an obstacle between them. And she saw herself, once her need to possess the man was satisfied, blurred into the background, confined to waiting for him, once again, and him barely justifying himself before leaving on new adventures.

Paul extracts another mug from a black-lacquered sliding drawer and makes the young woman some tea before returning to the table and resuming his work in progress. His face displays an expression of contentment, and Ema's presence seems to give him a feeling of security, for his movements are milder and slower than usual. This reaction reassures the young woman of her lover's genuine feelings and also surprises her, as she's surprised every time Paul drops his guard a little and gives her a glance at the place she occupies in his life.

From where she's sitting, Ema's eyes fall on a window set in the wall above the Corian countertop, in the corner of the fitted kitchen. As she tries to evoke a mental image of what their life together might be like, she pictures a repetition of the domestic scene they're living through right now, a scene Paul seems to find satisfying: the two of them, working side by side, while the shade of the cedar and the feeble light of fall days strain to pass through that window.

Then, all of a sudden, the image she's evoking strikes her as boring. This kitchen area, these partition walls inside upper-middle-class houses, are emblematic of the comfortable lifestyle that was already provided for her in her parents' home and that her husband's profession continues to make possible. Paul at home isn't showing her anything new. It's as though her lover, whom she selected for his licentious inclinations and who, she hoped, would assist her in transgressing the boundaries of her conformist, run-of-the-mill existence, has proved unqualified to help her evolve beyond the same petty-bourgeois world she's always known.

No, this is not where I want to join him, Ema thinks, and the revelation teaches her something new about the limits she herself needs to put on this affair. Up until the present moment, she's been too often hypnotized by Paul's boundaries, constantly running up against the obstacle presented by his wife.

Having formulated this truth in her head, she feels a disconnect with her lover, who's tenderly gazing at her, savoring, or so she imagines, his fantasy of an in-house, on-call Ema. She even starts to feel guilty at the idea of having feelings different from his. Then doubt returns to torment her and she wonders about Paul, who, after all, is more than capable of having staged this whole production.

"There's a chance my wife will come home," he tells her calmly, interrupting her musings.

His wife's a special-needs educator, the man explains, and she's currently assigned to the same *commune* they live in. As he tells Ema this, Paul is strangely, uncharacteristically calm. The imprecision of the information he's just given her contributes to making the threat of an embarrassing confrontation with his wife even vaguer. *Where can she be right now? In a nearby neighborhood, maybe? In this one?*

As Ema's vacillating, uncertain what to do next, the sound of the vacuum cleaner in the next room grows louder, the idea that there's a third party in the house suddenly recurs to them, and it's swiftly followed by the awareness that they're in a place where many restrictions apply: they can't touch each other; their conversation must remain impersonal. Nevertheless, this is the moment Paul chooses to put his hand on the young woman's knee.

"You know there's also a strong physical component in my attraction to you."

They gaze at each other for a moment, equally disconcerted. Paul looks awkward, as if embarrassed by his virility and apologizing to his mistress for it. Then the cleaning lady finally enters the room, and Ema decides to seize the opportunity to slip away. The man accompanies her to the door, and there, so he won't be overheard, murmurs in her ear, "Keep shaking me up. Deep down, I think that's what I really need."

the corner behind the front door
of ema's house at 7:30 in the evening

In the weeks following Ema's visit to her lover, her
anger rises to the surface again. To get some reaction
from Paul, she decides to push him into taking risks
at her house, on her own territory.

The fact is that he persists in meeting her only
in settings that are pretty safe for him, primarily the
young woman's house. The deceptive intimacy they
find there plunges her into a state of confusion and
makes her lose her bearings. When she and Paul meet

in her home, Ema's role as a wife and mother prohibits her physically and even psychologically from giving herself entirely. In hindsight, she assesses her attempt to get closer to Paul under his own roof and in the presence of his cleaning lady as a provocation on her part.

Her knowledge of the life he leads when he's not with her has recently grown far too specific. Busily juggling his obligations, Paul has little time to spare for her. His delays on construction sites, his problems hiring replacements, and his childhood friend's romantic tribulations seem to have acquired permanent status in his life.

Does he take me for a concubine? Ema sometimes wonders. *The cleverest of them all, the one who counsels the master?*

Taking advantage of her son's absence—he's at his grandmother's—the young woman arranges a meeting at her home late one afternoon with Paul and some other people. The purpose of the meeting is to set up a local branch of the Human Rights League.

During the working session, Paul appears genuinely stimulated by their new project, and Ema registers the efforts he seems willing to make in order to extend their collaboration beyond the term of his mandate at the labor court. The intense looks they exchange, as well as her lover's recent invitation to shake up his life, encourage the young woman and reinforce her determination to keep him with her after the meeting adjourns, even though her husband's due home from work before too long.

As the others are leaving, Ema tells Paul matter-of-factly, "I've got something I want to go over with you," thus flouting one of his rules of prudence: *Don't arouse suspicions by unusual behavior in the presence of witnesses.*

He hesitates, surprised by Ema's sudden proposal, before finally settling back into his chair. As soon as the door closes on the last attendee, they embrace in a corner of the entryway. Utterly forgetting himself, yielding to his emotions for once, he hugs the young woman tighter and tighter.

The fact that he's agreed to take this unusual step with her, to break with their usual routine, which leads them from the dining room table to the corner in the kitchen, is a first sign of rule-breaking to come. The sighs of relief coming from Paul disclose his impatience, as if he too, for once, feels the same urgency she does.

The venue they've chosen for reciprocal squeezing offers a deceptive level of security, even if they are indeed safe from being seen. They're just inside the front door, in a space a little more than one meter square, opening onto the dining room, bounded on one side by a closet containing a bucket, some brooms, and an electricity meter, and on the other by the garage wall. This space constitutes a sort of air lock that you pass through before really penetrating to the inside of the house. It's surrounded by wood: the solid wood of the door, the driftwood key holder on the opposite wall, the revolving pinewood panels of the closet. There are also elements at variance with the harmony of wood: light brown floor tiles, an acrylic glass lampshade, and the fanlight in the front door, through which you can get a look at the topmost lilac branches.

The space in question barely gets included in calculations of the house's square footage. The thickness of the front door is all that separates the little corner from the outside. So scanty is the area that no one can occupy it for any length of time, not even to slip on a pair of boots, and it would likewise be rude to test guests' patience by leaving them standing there too long. It's a trivial place, a place where you could find a scarf lying abandoned on the floor, heavy key rings hanging from their holder, a bread bag carelessly leaned against the wall.

The ringing of the telephone brutally yanks them out of their incautious rapture. Ema instantly realizes that the caller must be her husband, eager to report to her about a professionally important meeting he's just left.

The young woman sees the incredulity in Paul's eyes as he recoils slightly. *What on earth am I doing here*, he seems to be thinking.

"So what do we do now?" the young woman asks, exploiting her lover's bewilderment and pressing her advantage.

The serious look on Paul's face makes her think he's going to pronounce some well-considered words and admit that their relationship has intensified, that it's crossed a threshold. But he chooses to avoid the question instead.

To assuage his fear and keep him from running away again, Ema tries to communicate her exhilaration to him, pulling him against her more and more intimately. With all the gentleness at her command, she strokes his face, her hand moving over his mouth and his lips.

The lamp with the acrylic glass shade is off, and the darkness of the square entryway facilitates their careless abandon. The front-door window has the merit of marking the hours; by contrast, the ambience of the dark recess they're in entails the disadvantage of making them lose all notion of time. Outside activity reaches them only in a fragmented way, through the panes of the fanlight. Should anyone open the door, Ema and Paul would be trapped in their corner, backed against the wall with no possibility of retreat.

When she opens her eyes again, the young woman can distinguish the silver hinges of the front door, which feature a faux-antique patina, the nick in the paint where the round knob of a closet panel often strikes the wall, and, above her head, the black plastic box containing the doorbell chime, which—it seems to her—she hasn't noticed before.

The noises from outside, the muffled song of a bird, the distant rumble of a passing train, barely penetrating into the house, help to maintain the illusion of a brand-new time, uncharted and untried.

Whereas Paul has always managed their schedule, determining, for example, the hour at which it's
prudent to go home to their respective spouses in
order not to arouse suspicion, this evening he seems
to have ceded his prerogative and handed over the
decision-making to the young woman, perhaps because of weakness, perhaps because he trusts her to
handle the matter on her own territory.

Although Ema is aware of the risk she's running,
there are so many barriers in their relationship that
she wants to get past at least one with Paul, namely
time. She feels a strong urge to "see" what's beyond
it. Maybe, if the man gives in and crosses that line
with her, he'll lower his guard concerning other matters as well and definitively shed his armor.

In romantic fashion, she views this transgres-
sion as an act of emancipation and a way of ascend-
ing to a new level of confidence and revelation, like
the adulterous couple in Louis Malle's film *The
Lovers*, who fall passionately in love over the course
of a single night.

More and more afflicted by their repeated separations, still looking for the continuity in her life that
she'd already hoped to create when she dragged Paul
into the chapel, Ema's testing the impermeability of

two spaces, the one where she carries on with her lover and the conjugal sphere, at the risk of causing those two worlds to collide.

In this configuration, the barricade formed by the door remains the sole element of discontinuity, the last rampart between inside and outside.

At 7:30, the evening bustle becomes more noticeable; the sound of the neighbor's car as he brusquely pulls into the drive in order to back into his parking spot and the rolling of garbage cans being hauled to a communal pickup point at an intersection some distance away for tomorrow's collection are but two signs warning of Ema's husband's imminent arrival.

Is he aware that his rival will be home soon? she wonders, trying to assess the solidity of her lover's resolutions. Paul may not share her need for continuity, he may be willing to settle for a stop-and-start relationship, but she knows he's capable of acting on impulse. And that's the idea she's playing with at this moment, when her whole body is signaling to her lover, *If you love me, take me away and keep me. Don't leave me in another's hands.*

Is Paul overwhelmed by the situation? Doesn't he stress his need for control so much because he knows he's prone to weakness, an intolerable character trait for a man who sees himself as a natural leader, someone others ought to be able to count on?

"Every time I've started this kind of relationship with someone," he says, pulling back a little and taking the young woman's face in his hands, "there have always been consequences—for me, for the people close to me, and for the person I was with."

Then, as gently as he sometimes knows how to be, he murmurs, "My darling," again and again, all the while stroking her hair. Ema registers the restrained affection in his rather tired voice, as if he were continuing to pardon her for her inexperience.

Snatches of conversation between two neighbors outside, chatting as they come home from work, reach Ema and Paul more clearly. The young woman suddenly pricks up her ears, all attention, but she doesn't yet hear the sound of her husband's voice.

Ema's being tugged at by two contradictory forces: a form of curiosity that's pushing her to find out just how far two people can go in this kind of relationship, like children testing their limits, and the necessity, despite everything, of maintaining a certain level of control.

She can't help imagining what comes next: her husband's return, the cries, the doors opening and closing, as in a vaudeville comedy show or a stage farce.

Is that really what she wants? To blow everything to bits, all at one go? But for what? Her visit to Paul's home is still vivid in her memory; she recalls her disappointment, especially the revelation that his house wasn't where she wanted to be with him. In the end, that last thought is the one that makes her back down.

"You have to leave, my husband will be home soon."

"Yes, of course," says Paul, straightening his jacket. "I don't know how I could have stayed so late."

He hesitates some more on the front threshold before finally taking leave of her, and his dithering gives Ema hope that their relationship has passed a turning point; from now on, she believes, it can never be the same again.

When her husband comes home from work ten minutes after Paul's departure, the house hasn't had enough time, it hasn't emptied out enough to welcome him properly, and on this evening, the noise the door makes when he opens it, and his call, which sounds a bit curt and a bit merry, as if his hurrying footsteps put the whole household on the alert—those things encounter the traces left by the long clinch Ema and her lover just shared, the square area in the entryway still heavy with their sighs of abandon, the last pause before they let each other go. The superposition of those two scenes, played out with only a brief interval between them, creates a shock wave that the young woman tries her best to absorb.

the country lane

After Paul leaves Ema's house, three long weeks will have to pass before she hears from him again.

In an oft-recurring dream during this period, she's lost somewhere in the depths of the places she knew in childhood, especially holiday apartments, and she tries to reach Paul by telephone, but in vain. Her need to get in touch with him is great, so she's delighted to have his number, the ultimate sesame, which must allow her to pass over the obstacles presented by geographical distance and her return to her younger days. But she can't manage to tap the numbers on her phone screen, either because she forgets them as she goes along, or because she types the wrong ones. When she wakes up, that feeling of helplessness stays with her.

"I was drifting and letting you drift," Paul will explain months later, when they're finally able to speak about this difficult time; he judges his behavior as rather shameful, and she retains the painful memory of having once again been banished to her solitude.

During this waiting period imposed by her lover, the young woman passes from doubt to hope.

Did she go too far with him by pushing him back to his last line of defense? Is their relationship compromised now, and through her fault? The fact that she's still very much in love with him makes the idea of her responsibility seem all the more intolerable to her.

She finds comfort in remembering the man's other, similarly lengthy absences and then allows herself to make various predictions, one of which is quite optimistic. Paul has withdrawn to do some thinking, and having understood that their relationship can't be viable unless it's organized, he is perhaps, at this very moment, trying to find them an apartment.

Not very far from Ema's house, there's a footpath with a rural feel; it winds along behind the houses and brings her to a bus stop located on the departmental road that separates her *commune* from Paul's.

The young woman likes to take this path, which parallels the conventional, thoroughly planned street that runs through her subdivision. The footpath is a sort of country lane, which begins beyond the last houses, near a truck-farm greenhouse run by a group of enthusiastic young growers.

In former days, back in the mid-1970s, Ema's neighborhood abounded in such bypasses and back ways; every cluster of houses was crisscrossed by pathways, "secret passages" that children had to take during the games they played. Someone had also told her that the yards of the houses weren't separated from one another back then, and that behind the houses there was an immense expanse of common land; on weekends, moped-riding youngsters would hurtle across it from one side to another. Those were the free, happy, early days, the days before the houses and their lots closed in on themselves (for the sake of security, for the sake of tranquility), annexing the pathways behind them and fencing off their grounds.

The thought of those golden days makes Ema daydream about the time when it was possible to take winding paths rather than roads laid out in straight lines, an age when men and women weren't as subject as they are today to the pressures of their professional lives, to the obligation of becoming ever more productive, which ruins your taste for play, saps your energy for it, and eliminates your availability to help others.

Would Paul have had more time to spare for her in those days? Would they have strolled, just the two of them, down this truant lane?

One day in the very beginning of her relationship with Paul, as she was stepping off a bus, her eyes were drawn by something on the other side of the departmental road, in the direction of the neighboring *commune*, where her lover lived: running between two buildings, a passageway with an entrance so narrow and weed-choked that it gave her hope of discovering a new path there.

She immediately took it into her head to explore that path, and after five or six hundred rather monotonous meters, walking between the windowless back walls of houses and other buildings, she finally reached a point where the landscape changed, displaying more variety than she'd expected.

The path continued as a sunken lane. On the right-hand side, the ground rose to a crest with houses built along it. It was an autumn day, and leaves were falling into the ditch, cohering into a thick, wet carpet, and undoubtedly making the path harder to walk on.

Ema wanted to go on to the end, and soon she came to the edge of a hamlet, which—as she realized, to her delight—constituted an alternate entrance to Paul's subdivision and a new way for her to get very close to her lover's house, but under cover.

Afterward, and particularly during her weeks of solitude, whether she's tormented by doubt or regaining hope, Ema often takes this alternative route to Paul's house.

———

At the midpoint of the walk, still in Ema's subdivision, there's a concrete bench near a partly collapsed wall, some empty bottles, and a little channel where a thread of dirty water trickles toward some railings. On the other side are the athletic fields attached to a psychiatric institution for children and teenagers. Circles on the ground mark the boundaries of the play areas. There are tall trees, plane trees, so numerous and so big that they create a zone of darkness on that part of the large property.

When Ema yields to discouragement and her house, her habitual place of refuge, can't hold her anymore, she sometimes lingers on that bench, lulling herself with the idea that Paul could join her there.

In the young woman's determination to remain mentally close to Paul, even in his absence, there's a concern for maintaining her level of desire, for staying inside this period of turmoil, which she pictures as movement, circular movement. It's imperative for her to remain in the eye of the storm. One single step aside, and their chance will have passed.

In the path's numerous twists and turns, Ema's apprehension of time and space alters, granting the young woman a plunge into an imagined world, a vision of what her relationship with Paul might have been like in other circumstances.

When Ema reaches the higher ground, she's still in the gully formed by the sunken lane; it's badly maintained all year round, and here it's an overgrown tangle of bushes and brambles, crowding in from both sides. Sometimes she thinks she's the last person who will ever use this path.

She likes to observe the sides of the houses she walks past; seen from this new viewpoint, they reveal previously invisible details: the arch of a rusty old swing set with the swings removed; the back of a dog kennel; a carpet of pine needles strewn over a driveway, giving the house the look of a forest chalet; a mostly unfinished treehouse.

Trivial though they are, these details have a certain mysterious aura, as if, as she proceeds along the path, the young woman were moving backward in time toward a sort of forgotten territory, whose rediscovery will be a gift given to her alone.

When she arrives near Paul's house, Ema refrains from getting too close to it, out of prudence, but also because she doesn't know whether he'd appreciate learning that she's been prowling around his home.

But maybe he'd simply prefer to close his eyes to the young woman's wanderings, provided she's available when he wants her.

With money left to him in an inheritance, the man had been one of the first to purchase a house in his subdivision. In those days, he was young, intermittently free, childless, and still unacquainted with the trauma of separations.

Buying that house had been an important milestone for him. He'd known immediately that the possession he'd just acquired would remain in his hands, even should other things in his life happen to crumble away.

"Keep an eye on my town while I'm gone," the lovers sometimes murmur to each other with a smile when one of them is about to take a vacation. They share, both of them, a very strong need to be anchored somewhere.

"If we'd met twenty-five years ago, I would have asked you to move in with me right away," the man declared one day, innocently, as the young woman was reproaching him for taking the situation too lightly. It was as if he hoped, by transposing their relationship to a different time period, to prove the sincerity of his commitment.

From time to time he'd allude, in veiled terms, to his life as a pretty dissolute young man, marked by the absence of his father, feeble motivation, and a few stupid mistakes; and then the resumption of his studies and, at last, the charting of a course, from which he hasn't deviated since. Now resolutely turned toward the future, intent on making up for lost time, Paul pretended to be unaware of the impact his talk about his past had on the young woman, the curiosity and the craving it awakened in her.

Ema paid careful attention to what Paul told her about the places he'd frequented in bygone days—the downstairs jazz clubs around the Hôtel de Ville, for example, one of which was always the last stop of his evenings out. A favorite spot was an exotic restaurant on rue de Faubourg-Saint-Antoine, where he would wine and dine women on the strength of his first pay-checks. His way of describing all that, the plethora of details, had particularly struck Ema. The establish-ment's Chinese-whorehouse look and its tawdry lux-ury. The owner, who always welcomed Paul like some sort of accomplice. The mirrors on the ceiling and the walls, reflecting amply proportioned Buddhas. The abundant green plants. The sound of flowing water from a fountain on the upper floor. The very special layout of the rooms. The couples sitting on circular benches, their thighs touching in mutual provocation. The waitress gliding from one table to another, placing flavorful dishes in front of customers: cilantro dumplings, sliced beef with onions, Peking duck.

Ema's always been attracted to men who like to stand out and live in high style. As a child on vacation on the Côte d'Azur, she was already fantasizing about boat owners and casino habitués, men who ogled beautiful and sophisticated women. She still remembers the woody scents of the colognes that pervaded her dreams for a long time.

That taste for the game is exactly what she feels capable of reviving in the man, just as she feels proud of herself, while strolling down the country lane, for rescuing an abandoned path, a trail she's sure even Paul has forgotten, from oblivion.

And this certainty of hers, this conviction that she has the ability to give her lover back his past, not only invests her with power but also, at the same time, grants her the confidence she needs to put up with waiting for the moment when he'll finally decide to come back to her.

the tearoom in the shopping mall

After three long weeks of silence, Paul calls up the young woman and arranges to meet her in a bakery in the shopping mall.

The tearoom in the bakery is boxlike, its area forty-nine square meters and its décor rustic, bounded on one side by a counter over a display case with products for takeout, and on the other by the adjoining shoemaker's shop, whose flashing red sign is reflected on all the glass surfaces. The back wall allows a glimpse of the bakery's kitchens, while the front of the room, except for a low latticework partition around a few tables, is wide open to the mall concourse. Across the way, customers congregate in front of a machine dispensing postal materials, using their credit cards to activate a magnetic arm that raises envelopes into the air and drops them down a chute.

In spite of the noise outside in the shopping mall, the marketing events and flash sales that occur intermittently, inside the bakery there's a regular hum produced by background music and the sound of a children's carousel.

The location of the tearoom—in a side passage, a few steps from one of the least used mall entrances—is such that it guarantees the lovers a relatively high degree of unobtrusiveness and tranquility. Most of the time, it's Ema who tends to choose this spot when she wants a neutral space unlikely to give rise to interfering emotions, a setting that will allow both of them to take a step back and gain some perspective on their relationship.

———————

A few people, not many, walk past: a family pushing a shopping cart, a couple of mall cops from the security office, out on patrol and carrying walkie-talkies. On the floor, in the midst of a sea of cheap marble, markers indicate the route to the mall's nerve center, which is situated some distance away; after a few turns, you come to a sort of island covered with rectangular blocks of what appears to be kryptonite, on the surface of which images of flowing water and effervescent bubbles are projected as a relaxing diversion for the shoppers who sit inside circles of the mottled gray carpet that defines the limits of the rest areas in the mall.

As a general rule, Ema and Paul meet in this tearoom in the morning and have breakfast here. The heavy wooden tables, arranged in straight lines, maintain a distance between the customers that's limited but sufficient to offer a modicum of privacy. The young woman who takes their orders is always very meticulous about her appearance and lends a touch of femininity to a place lacking in warmth, a place whose rather unlovely ambiance, with its harsh lights shining down from a false ceiling, seems more appropriate for business meetings than for romantic assignations. This is a plus for Paul and Ema, who wish to fade into a certain anonymity.

But despite the hubbub surrounding them, their words stand out and make them conspicuous. The sounds of the mall, the conversations of the other customers, envelop the lovers and contain them.

"How are you?" Paul asks as he sits down. He puts the question in a tone of forced enthusiasm, eager to erase his weeks of absence and silence as quickly as he can; his sudden solicitude and more or less artificial way of listening to her upset Ema. It's as though he's pretending to open a time slot in his crowded schedule, but the opening's too narrow to allow the young woman to get a word in.

In any case, Paul's question was merely rhetorical, because he starts talking right away. He explains to Ema that he's done a lot of thinking, and that he accepts his share of responsibility for the reckless behavior that took place at her house and the ill-considered risk they ran. He acknowledges that his lack of availability and the fact that he always leaves the young woman wanting more, sexually and otherwise, were bound to lead to bad behavior. That's why, he concludes, he's reserved an apartment for them in a residential hotel one day next week.

Paul has rarely spoken about their relationship at such length. He seems happy, almost relieved, to see Ema again. The young woman's delighted that he's decided to take things in hand, but she's sorry that his proposal of an ephemeral tryst doesn't carry his reasoning through to its logical conclusion.

Made confident by Paul's implications and longing to recapture the emotion of their last meeting, she ventures to ask him, lowering her voice, if she's his "soul mate."

There are few other customers around them this early in the morning, and those who are present are, for the most part, regulars, including two supervisors from the mall's big department store, treating themselves to a last cup of coffee before a hiring session, and, leaning with his back against the counter, the boyfriend of one of the waitresses.

As he often does, Paul replies to the young woman's question with a "Yes..." of agreement and a bit of throat-clearing, his way of gaining time, and then he falls silent. When he's ready to reply to her, Ema figures, he'll pick up an object, a sugar cube or a piece of silverware, and examine it with care before delicately rolling it around in his fingers.

When they're having an important conversation, the man often indulges in this odd habit, and his movements, as well as the effort he then puts into stressing his words and making sure they're getting through, support the young woman's idea that their relationship is deepening, even if he invariably ends by saying, "You're the one who's good with words, not me," as an apology for his response, which he considers lame, or as a way of protecting the part of him that will remain in shadow.

"I wouldn't use that expression," the man replies. "I've learned not to be dependent on anyone, not even in love."

As Ema, stunned speechless, keeps her gaze fixed on him, he opts, with a certain annoyance, for dodging. "Don't ask me to give you a more satisfactory answer to that question," he says. "I have no intention of analyzing what's hidden in my depths, like what part my upbringing played in all this. I won't do it."

Later, the young woman will try to recall each of the terms Paul used.

At the moment, she's mostly struck by the rather harsh and impersonal tone he employs to respond to her.

All at once, the very small distance that separates the lovers seems like a practically unbridgeable gap that prevents them from mitigating the insult with physical contact, a gesture that would have been possible in more intimate surroundings, such as a hotel room, for example, or the interior of the man's car.

Ema, who hasn't had breakfast yet, feels the beginnings of an anxiety attack, a disorder that afflicts her from time to time. Her vision starts to blur and Paul's outline recedes, while the bakery's walls close in on her, making it harder for her to breathe. To calm herself, she holds tight to the table, disguising her distress so as not to worry her lover.

The man's coldness has, oddly enough, projected itself onto the surrounding décor, suddenly revealing all of its fake, industrial components. The staircase in the center of the room that rises to a landing with an observation railing and some false exits. The half-open door in the back, through which you can enter a bare, dark corridor that links one store to another and offers workers a bolt-hole to disappear into briefly, absorbed by their cigarettes, their commercial smiles instantaneously gone from their faces. Sheaves of dried wheat placed on metal watering cans, molds in animal shapes, grape presses, rakes, and other replicas of agricultural implements, all covered with dust.

For a long time, Ema has thought she's conjured up an acceptable niche inside this violently standardized corporate environment, has believed she's found a unique spot to which her meetings with Paul give a particular cast, a place that allows her a chance to catch her breath. The fact that they could transform such an unremarkable venue as this bakery into a propitious setting was proof that she was right.

Was she mistaken? Is Paul just another consumer, nourishing himself on the emotions of their relationship? Is the man really there, sitting next to her in this tearoom?

Then the symptoms of the young woman's anxiety fade slowly away, and her surroundings start to slip back into place. Especially because Paul, who has fallen on his breakfast, has also noticed her unsettled state, and now he makes an effort to comfort her, with words that are pretty awkward but nonetheless affectionate.

"I love your take on things," or "Your way of looking at the world is indispensable to me." Certain of her lover's declarations, pronounced in solemn tones at some point in the past, return to her memory as she comes to her senses.

"Am I your soul mate?"—questions requiring such committed answers should be reserved for very special places, Ema thinks, regretting that she let herself be taken in by this phony décor. *If not, the setting where they're asked can only distort them.* She ought to know, however, that Paul's coldness is seldom a display of strength or detachment, but rather an expression of fragility. Of vulnerability, which today is inducing him to lie deliberately in order to protect himself and calm things down; the young woman's convinced of that now.

A ray of light that has managed to pass through who knows where falls on their table, illuminating the scene. It's a brief moment of grace that recalls to Ema the joy of hearing what Paul implied a little while ago, when he told her about the hotel and invited her to take the plunge.

"I'm positively amazed by your ability to maintain this kind of relationship over time," Paul told her once, and she felt proud of the extraordinary power—to accept secrecy and succeed in working around it—that he attributed to her.

And it's this gratifying image of herself that Ema wants to keep before her lover's eyes. She's quite determined to prove to him that she's strong and ready to embark on a long-term relationship with him now that he's taken a step toward her and invited her to join him in a new place, a place outside the circle of their daily lives.

apartment hotel

"Appart'hôtel." Atop a modern building, a gray and blue logo displays the name of the establishment, which has recently sprung up on land where a former inventory clearance warehouse and a bowling alley used to stand side by side. Neat little brick walls, colonies of young shrubs in the center of a vast parking lot—the approach to the apartment hotel looks like the circuits that schools set up on their playgrounds to raise awareness concerning road safety.

———

The reception counter, a boat-hull-shaped combination of stainless steel and blond pinewood, is as big as the entire lobby of an average apartment building. A sofa covered with brown fabric has been placed in a corner. "Park Activities," says the hotel's advertising slogan, but it's hard to know exactly what sort of activities are meant. The man behind the counter has been a hotel clerk for a few hours. Sheets can be picked up and paid for the day before.

Paul is spared these "arrangements." It falls to Ema to confront the incidentals first and deal with them. "A woman's life is a life of details," Ema's mother used to say. She, Ema, is the only one available at that particular moment. Also the only one to wonder whether the apartment Paul has reserved is suitable for habitation.

Rows of mailboxes along one wall of the lobby. They can have their own little lock-up garage, like the other residents. They can make love like a legitimate couple, but in broad daylight.

The interior of the apartment, the fittings and fixtures, are Spartan. The single large, open area serves as both bedroom and living room. The furniture has been reduced to the essential minimum: four chairs with wooden backs and dark green fabric seats; a round white fairly low table; a double bed whose mattress cover is decorated by two bands of slightly faded green and yellow material with patterns of pastoral scenes; a set of plywood shelves; and, on the wall above a sofa bed, a panoramic picture of a field of sunflowers. On the right as you enter the door, a kitchenette with a sink, a single cooking surface, a little countertop, a dishwasher, and a fridge, all fitted together as tidily as possible to form one neat rectangular block.

This setting suits Ema just fine: its arid neutrality allows her to free herself from her wifely and maternal ties and make herself totally available to Paul.

The room gives her a momentary sensation of floating between the land and the sea. The residence is set back from the quays of the Seine, leaving the river's water to flow on the other side of the street, maybe beyond the reach of melancholy.

The mid-afternoon sun, tempered by the Dacron curtain that covers the big picture window, bathes the interior. The color of the fabric, which tends toward yellow, diffuses a smoky light around the room. When she opens the window, Ema sees the back of the building. A patch of inaccessible lawn. Other apartments across from the one she's in. Ventilation grilles.

The young woman is surprised at how easily she gets through this interim period. After she makes the bed, she sits on a chair, preferring not to leave the apartment.

In the hospital where her mother was undergoing treatment, a room had been made available for patients' families, but Ema refused to stay there alone in the afternoon. The feeling that her existence was empty, a void she had yet to fill with anything of her own devising, was bound to catch up with her in that vacant space, bound to seize the opportunity to overwhelm her. A row of windows at the back of the building encircled the visitors' room, and into that room, through a gap between the roofs, a white light was projected. Its brightness was as pale as medicine; she imagined it capable of dissolving her.

By contrast, the emptiness here seems promising. It recalls to her memory other periods of time spent waiting, but happily.

Her last babysitter, with whom her mother sometimes left her overnight, lives in an apartment within easy walking distance from here. Ema thinks about the window overlooking the Seine, a small, badly insulated little square of wood, and sees herself standing in front of it on cold feet, as she so often did, pressing her forehead against the glass pane. The static image of the Seine, that slow, industrious river, ferrying merchandise along, its quays little used, disappointed the child she was, like an unkept promise of the sea. The sight of it, however, held her eyes. It was as if that immobility and that calm had the power to make something appear.

The room she'd had for a week while attending a seminar in Bruges sometime after she was married overlooked a canal. It was winter, and the water was icy. The room was tailor-made for a single person and seemed to strive toward perfect unity. Single bed, closet, little shower capsule. The noise, amplified by the empty corridor, of the magnetic door slamming shut. No television, but a radio on the nightstand.

The little blackout curtain that she pulled down to just above the desk. She'd never inhabited a space so well. Did she already feel the need for a lover back then, despite that perfection? Like something that gnaws at you inside a little, a nagging desire? She inscribed some names on the misted windowpane.

Starting tomorrow, everything must be new, Ema tells herself. Paul's going to come and join her, and then he'll take her in his arms. The sex will immediately allow them to let go, to set free the emotions they've kept in check too long. She expects this experience to be a revelation.

Upon leaving, she says good-bye to the man on duty, embarrassed because it's so easy for him to guess why she and her lover have rented the apartment. But the clerk's busy filling out papers and completely indifferent to her, and the young woman, even though she's relieved to be able to pass unnoticed, can't help judging modern times, when employees are trained to stay out of everyone's business: *As long as the money keeps coming in...*

The next morning, Ema's the first to arrive, but Paul soon rings the doorbell. When the door closes behind him, the calm of the beginning of the day, the fact of occupying an apartment rather than a room, and the distance between her and home comfort the young woman in the idea that she's burned some bridges.

The man turns off his cell phone, declining to give regular reports, accepting the idea that he's taking a risk. Ema finds this gesture highly arousing; she feels they're switching over together to a new time, a somewhat troubling, boundless time, a break with the in-between period they've known thus far. Behind the silence, the young woman can almost hear, but in a muffled way, the furious noises of those who might be looking for them, who might be outside, getting all worked up, frantic to penetrate the space she and her lover have absented themselves in.

Once the door's safely closed again, Paul comes to the young woman to take her in his arms. The narrow entrance hall compels them to lean against the counter in the recessed kitchenette.

For the occasion, Ema has bought a new, fairly close-fitting dress, under which she's wearing nothing at all, her lover having one day revealed to her his fantasy of discovering her naked under her clothes. Paul, who always starts delicately with her, doesn't immediately notice, and she savors in anticipation the pleasure that the discovery will bring him. When he realizes what he's up against, it's so exciting for both of them that it practically takes their breath away. Never until this moment has Ema felt so like a woman; that is, so correspondent in all points to the image of femininity she's made for herself: participating in a staged desire that gives off a heady scent of danger. When tension builds, as it's building today, she has the sense that the childish roundness of her features—the impression she gives of dozing a little, which has persisted even after her pregnancy—disappears all at once.

Their embrace continues, and Ema thinks that the moment so hoped for has come at last, that it has just been delayed by various obstacles, constraints of time and place, and that Paul has longed for it as much as she has, in spite of certain perfectly legitimate qualms.

The man's the one who breaks their clinch first. "Look, I got the croissants," he says enthusiastically, pulling off his tie.

Because Paul proposes making some coffee, Ema's obliged to busy herself alongside him, and she searches for necessary items in the cabinets.

This interruption gives her time to take a closer look at the layout of the kitchenette: the sink, a sheet of aluminum so thin that she could put her finger through it, and its backsplash, consisting of square white tiles embellished by a central line of bottle-green tiles in relief.

While they take their seats at the table to have their breakfast, Ema strives feverishly to understand the reasons why Paul's postponing their lovemaking. Is it perhaps that he's not comfortable with programmed moments of intimacy and needs to take his time, particularly when it comes to desiring her, or is it just the opposite, and he's trying to calm his impatience?

Against all expectation, the man leans back comfortably in his chair and starts telling her about the latest developments in the ongoing drama of his best friend and his problems, as relaxed as if he and Ema were in his car. Ema stays quiet, crushed by the idea that the moment she's been so ardently waiting for, perhaps one of their last chances, is passing, profaned by Paul's opening moves. At first timidly, and then more explicitly, she strokes her lover's leg in an attempt to raise the temperature. As he keeps talking, they finally move closer together, until the man suggests that they cross over to the bed.

Paul removes his jacket and drapes it over the back of a chair. He's elegantly dressed, and Ema thinks he looks quite handsome. But he continues to control the space they're in with the same methodical calm, taking the time to lay his watch perfectly flat on the nightstand.

Then he finally joins her on the bed and raises her dress. She lets him have his way with her as he licks her breasts and his hands slide up between her thighs. His movements are slow and conscientious, as if he were still holding his desire in check, playing for time.

The young woman has often imagined this moment, and now that it's here, she feels something like indifference, like absence from the unfolding scene. Her head is clear, and on the one hand, she can visualize all the elaborate fantasies she's built up around her desire, and on the other, she can see Paul and herself, here on the bed, but she can't, despite her efforts, manage to connect the two sights.

Paul lies on top of her, and at last she gets excited, aroused particularly by his way of raising her legs a little higher at each thrust to penetrate her more deeply. But he comes quickly, and her frustration is meticulously accompanied by renewed desire.

Ema's very disappointed at having once again missed what she was aiming for, and she wonders if she's responsible for that, or if her lover has purposely speeded things up, careful as usual not to get carried away by his feelings. Inside her body, desire forms a hard, hot point whose intense force chokes her up a little and prevents her from talking freely with Paul. There's a hemorrhagic component in her craving. Should her lover want to take her again, something might come pouring out.

As for the man, he seems quite at his ease, doesn't bother to put anything on before wandering around the room, and even leaves the bathroom door wide open. But this natural behavior holds no mystery for the young woman and doesn't constitute the "laying bare" she's been expecting.

Although Paul's often inattentive, even he can't help noticing the furrow of vexation in Ema's forehead. *I'm going to try to open up a new space for us*, the man announced in the tearoom. He'll blame himself for this failed effort later, but on the grounds that he erred in not going far enough.

"I should have given up everything to have what we could have had together, you and I, but you see, I didn't have the right to do that," the man will say to Ema again.

Now that they've made love, the young woman doesn't know what to do with the time remaining in their rendezvous. Paul has reserved the room for the whole day.

The place they have at their disposal has lost its usefulness for her, and the crass décor has become unbearable. She'd like to move up their checkout time, but she's still wondering how to utilize the space next to the bed, the living room area with its television and its couch. Eventually, that's where the man will choose to sit for a while before leaving at the end of their encounter, with Ema on his lap, like a little girl.

the novotel by the lake

The day after their unsatisfactory tryst, it continues to intrigue Ema, who replays over and over in
her mind that very short moment of arousal, right
after Paul arrived, when she'd been afraid of the new
phase they were shifting into and had felt more like a
woman than she'd ever felt before, a moment thrill-
ing enough to help her put her ensuing disappointment into perspective.

She winds up convincing herself that the state of abandon she's sought so diligently with Paul was certainly close at hand, within their reach, and that perhaps it might be enough for them to re-create that instant of carnal agitation in order to get another chance.

Three weeks later, she proposes to meet her lover not in a neutral setting, but right in the middle of one of her fantasies, in a room in the Novotel in the Parisian suburb of Créteil. For a long time when she was a child, that city, a perpetual worksite, incarnated for her the idea of an elsewhere that filled her head with dreams.

Novotel, "New Hotel." She seems to remember that the first in the chain, the one she stayed in with her parents when she was a little girl, was located amid vineyards, somewhere in the vicinity of Perpignan. Square plexiglass key ring. The smell of newness, associated with an idea of futurity. "They surely have a swimming pool," Ema's mother had told her.

She can still remember her father, slipping into bed between smooth sheets in the middle of the day. Octagonal windows. Her mother, drawing the net drapes for a siesta, like closing the curtains in a capsule.

These memories transport the young woman to a time past and gone, a time when her parents were still around. A simple, stripped-down elsewhere, reflected in the décor of the room, where her mother, in her short-skirted 1970s minidress, stretched up on tiptoe to reach a curtain.

The land where the Créteil Novotel stands today used to be a large tract of open ground; then an artificial lake was created on the site, and only afterward did the construction of the hotel begin. Architecturally innovative buildings, like stalks of Brussels sprouts with diamond-shaped balconies in every imaginable color, have sprung up from the earth all around the hotel site. Spreading urbanization has encircled it, confining it to a small island of land that only a highway and an embankment now separate from the town.

Like a mirror reflecting other mirrors, the placid surface of the lake reflects the glass façades of the surrounding buildings.

Ema's five years old. She's with her parents, and they've arrived at a place whose location is unknown to her, there to check the progress of the work on an apartment they bought before construction began. In front of her is a vast expanse of land and, placed at the four corners of this grandiose space, various pieces of construction machinery, like the cardinal points on a compass. A man is holding some documents in one hand and pointing to something in the distance with the other. The scene makes a deep impression on the little girl; it's as if she were taking her first steps on the moon.

But years go by, and the visit is never repeated. Her parents' lives continue on their ordinary course. Ema hears only occasional echoes from that other place—the studio apartment her parents are furnishing as a rental property, the tenants moving in or out in an unending dance. The name of Créteil always evokes for her a tangle of lines and curves, an unfinished space, a geometry of elsewhere.

At the reception counter, a magnetic badge has supplanted the plexiglass key ring. In the room, the smell of a fresh duvet. Your home away from home. The idea of futurity has been replaced by a standardized, comfortable present. The net drapes of her memories are gone, and blackout curtains in various shades of beige are in their stead; she opens the curtains halfway. There's a view of the town and its buildings in the distance, and of the parking lot down below.

In fact, Paul's approaching the hotel through that lot, looking worried, pausing for a few moments before taking the plunge and entering the building, as Ema's already seen him do on one or two other occasions. Now she's amused by the thought of him standing immobile in front of the door, keeping his emotions under control or maybe trying to compose his features, the way you pass a hand over your face before you start a new undertaking.

Ten minutes after shutting himself up in the bathroom, the man calls to Ema to come and join him.

The bathroom is bigger than the young woman remembers. In addition to the tub, she sees now that there are twin washbasins, a big mirror illuminated by two obliquely placed, torch-shaped sconces, and, for storage, several gray lacquered drawers fitted with stainless steel pulls.

To please Paul, Ema came to their previous rendezvous naked under her dress; today it's his turn to make an effort to satisfy one of her fantasies.

"You always wanted a man to wash your hair," he tells her, pointing to the bathtub, whose pure lines are no longer hidden by the wooden casing that was combined with teal-colored plastic floor covering in the 1970s.

The man snatches away the towel he tied around his waist after washing up, revealing the concave belly below his muscular torso. Ema can't help reading his recent weight loss as an outward sign of the inner turmoil caused by their liaison. "Are you sleeping well? Have you been drinking more alcohol than before?" Paul often asks her, as if it were possible to maintain control in this sort of relationship by focusing on health-related considerations.

The young woman takes off her clothes and bends her body a little to make room for her lover, who kneels behind her, holding the shower head in one hand, and turns the faucets affixed to the bathtub, unlike the jet block that used to be located under the sink in the old days and that operated both the bath and the shower.

"You like it like that?" the man asks, slowly massaging Ema's hair.

"Yes," she replies, abandoning herself to his hands.

The young woman's eyes slide over the large charcoal-gray tiles that cover the bathroom wall, looking for the tiles she remembers: small, glazed, mostly pale beige. She can still recall the pattern they formed, two vertical columns of a darker brown and, in the space between those strips of color, a random scattering of tiles, like a jumble of agitated atoms. Her gaze lingers on the big mirror, and her memories surge up with even greater force.

During her stay at the hotel with her parents, she examined the bathroom in great detail, searching for the tiniest crack, for a rough edge, something that could offer a passage, a way out, an escape, and she told herself stories—for example, that the round inside doorknob could turn all by itself, and that someone, man or woman, was going to spring through the door and fondle her.

Superimposing the two images—Ema as a child in the bathroom of the 1970s Novotel, and the present Ema, naked before her lover—arouses the young woman, giving her almost as much pleasure as Paul's desire, openly demonstrated at last, to fulfill her fantasies.

Nevertheless, she senses that the man's watching her, observing her, lying in wait for her reactions, and the way he's doing it ends up making her uncomfortable.

"Being observant is the most important quality a salesman can have," her lover declared to her one day, hamming up the role of company chairman, which he followed with an entire discourse on customer relations. A customer must be a captive, he proceeded to explain to her. Displeasing him or her is to be avoided at all costs; otherwise, the captive breaks free, and then you have to start all over again, from the beginning.

This cynical view of romantic relationships as based solely on an alignment of interests seriously depresses the young woman.

Now the hot water's running over Ema's hair, over her face. Paul asks her to stand up so he can give her a thorough rinsing.

"I can't tell you what an effect it has on me to see you like this, without any clothes on, right next to me," the man says. "Basically, I think the vulnerability of women turns me on."

Paul admits to her, in a neutral tone and without exhibiting any guilty feelings, that he's behaved dishonestly in the past. He offers one example, involving his second-to-last partner, whom he'd left inconsolable, her eyes streaming with tears, on the day of their breakup, just turned on his heels and left her in the middle of the apartment, like a real bastard, running away from his sudden desire to make love to her.

The young woman loves listening to Paul talk about his past. Once he starts, his memories come tumbling out in disorder, liberated by logorrhea, as if he's lived several lives, each of which ended fairly abruptly, but he's never afterward taken the time to think them over.

Those anecdotes stimulate Ema's imagination. One by one, she pictures the women, parading them before her mind's eye like so many action figures. She manipulates them easily, because they come with obvious, uncomplicated personality traits. Some are total strangers to her, but to others she lends feelings that could be her own and feels sorry for them. Sometimes she imagines a chronology for Paul, based on his movement from conquest to conquest. After their separation, she'll still take this mental path from time to time, as if doing so could give her the missing keys or maybe shed some light on something.

She wonders if Paul really understands exactly what her fantasy is about. What has he gathered from it? Does he realize that when they have the chance to discuss their respective pasts, their conversation flows freely, excitingly?

To find out, the young woman takes the risk of explaining her feelings. She talks about the bathroom mirror, which—like Alice's mirror in Lewis Carroll's story—has just served as a passageway for her, a portal to the time of her childhood, when she was wedged between the couple formed by her parents and inwardly longing for "the other," for a masculine presence. She tries to describe how she'd like to go farther and farther back and bring to light her original emptiness, the one that arouses desire. She even goes so far as to describe to him her walks along the country lane, which like the mirror is capable of distorting her impressions of time and space.

Paul listens to her without a word; he doesn't share his own experience of child-parent relations. It appears that he's letting himself be lulled by the sound of Ema's voice. Charming though this attitude of devotion may be, it eventually reduces the young woman to silence.

"You know, I'm a simple man," he says by way of apology to the disappointed Ema, who concludes that her lover, as she feared, isn't ready to involve himself totally with her; he's mostly just trying to make up for their last failed encounter.

And now, look, he starts running his hands over her. Then he bends down and presses his face between her legs. While he's tasting her sex, Ema feels her body tensing, then her fists clenching, in anticipation of approaching, imminent pleasure.

I suppose he wants repayment in kind, she thinks cynically, after he makes her come. This bookkeeping reaction, which isn't like her, immediately saddens the young woman and revives in her a powerful sensation of solitude. As far as emotions are concerned, her affair with Paul hasn't exactly been infusing her with energy lately; it's been draining it out of her.

A quarter of an hour later, the man, having already stayed too long, has to dash away, leaving Ema, who's in less of a hurry, to finish getting dressed and to deal with the disorder they've made. He pauses on the threshold for a moment, quite obviously worried, as if the sensation of a cleft between him and his mistress has disturbed him too, and in such circumstances he deems it an increasingly risky proposition to leave behind him the idea of his absence.

After he goes, the young woman compels herself to gather her thoughts in the middle of the space she and Paul, it seems, have once again not tried hard enough to close up together.

the turnstile

In the heart of Paul's neighborhood, there's a block of three small apartment buildings, with single houses built around them. Some businesses—pharmacy, bakery, minimart—have gradually moved in at their feet, and the end result is a mini–shopping center that offers the advantage of being open on Sundays.

To reach the center, you have to park in a lot laid out for this purpose and walk past a group of houses to a narrow alley that leads to the square with all the shops. To prevent shoppers from driving their cars through the subdivision, the alley has been closed to vehicular traffic, including motorcycles, it's studded with speed bumps, and one stretch of it narrows to a turnstile. This has never been replaced or repaired, and its horizontal crossbars, which rusted and seized up not long after it was installed, forces pedestrians to contort their bodies in order to get past it.

On the right, just before you enter the alley, is one end of Paul's street. From this intersection, you can glimpse the front of the man's car if he's home, a tiny part of his roof, mostly hidden by a tree, the white-painted soffit board, and two of the three columns that support the projecting portion of the roof.

Seen from this spot, the various façades and their component parts—doors, windows, garage entrances—blend together into a confused mass, as if the houses on the street ultimately formed a single, unique dwelling with a practically infinite number of openings.

Ema occasionally comes to this neighborhood to do some shopping on Sundays or during the holidays.

Over the course of her affair with Paul, she would
never fail to turn her head to the right as she ap-
proached the intersection near the alley. The excuse
of running errands authorized her to glance over at
her lover's house while at the same time allowing her
to keep her distance. As she turned into the alley, her
step became lighter at the mere thought that the man
might notice her and maybe even come and join her.
But as she drew near the turnstile, a sort of indeci-
siveness would take hold of her, a loss of motivation
to continue on her way.

Ema and Paul never went back to the Novotel in
Créteil. In the following months, their meetings were
just as intermittent as before, until the young woman
decided to end their affair.

The man had spoken to her about a friend's
apartment in Paris that was going to be available and
that he was thinking about subletting. But Ema explained that it was too late for that now, their time
had passed, her desire was gone.

Ultimately, the lessons she'd drawn from Paul's
responses to her questions, their divergent views
of a romantic relationship, views that admitted no

possibility of adjustment, her longing for an ideal space where she could be one with her lover, and all the things she'd thought but never had the occasion to tell him—the young woman had chosen to keep all that to herself.

She also kept, and treasured, the feeling that she'd gained some freedom through discovering with him a space/time that belonged only to her, and that she had to make a special effort to keep open, without yielding to the sorrow of not seeing her lover anymore or to the temptation of retreating into herself and shutting out everything else.

He'd recalled aloud their first discussions, which had caused them to linger too late in his car, and spoken of the urge he'd sometimes felt to flip Ema onto her back, right there on the seat, so he could kiss her. But then, he wondered, where would he have taken her?

Other considerations, assuming they rented an apartment, were the consequences such an investment would have on his family life, as well as the fear that he wouldn't be capable of occupying the place sufficiently to satisfy Ema. All these issues had paralyzed him.

After their separation, going to Paul's neighborhood
to do her shopping takes on, for the young woman,
the nature of a test.

It snows the winter they break up. Basic, concrete, soot-blackened chimney stacks protrude, snugly
snow-capped, from the roofs of the houses all around;
smoke and the smell of burning wood spew from the
chimneys. The snowflakes swirling in the air recall to
Ema her own feeling of fragmentation and confer on
the scene the false sweetness of a world in which all
sound seems to have been absorbed.

When there's some movement near the man's
house, a car driving off, the silhouette of a person
leaving the house, Ema struggles to maintain control
of her emotions, suddenly assaulted, as in the past,
by a barrage of questions: *Who's in his house? Does he
have guests? How long will they stay?*

But she doesn't take the full measure of her mis-
ery until after she's walking in the alley, jammed
between the low sky like a leaden cloak and the chi-
canes, which curve around concrete triangles embed-
ded in the ground and decorated in the center with
spindly shrubs. The turnstile at the end looks to her
like one of those ritual places that manga heroines
with backpacks and short skirts and grimacing faces

must pass through recurrently, at different seasons, before they can break free of the cycle.

By the time a few months pass, the fascination of Paul's house has started to diminish.

On certain evenings, when she's walking through that alley on her way home from shopping, she sees the last rays of the setting sun lighting up the group of houses that includes Paul's.

From a distance, the alignment of his car and the houses, or the arc described by an opening door, seems stylized, and even the outlines of people no longer look human but rather like the stick figures that children draw crudely and that always make you wonder if they're full-face or in profile.

The signs of demarcation between the houses, the little thickets and low walls, stand out more clearly and resemble the miniature elements of scenery people use as accessories in electric train sets.

A wind seems to have swept over the neighborhood, making everything in its path dry as a bone, redrawing the picture but without the flesh. Nonetheless, there's one precise, particular point, one protrusion, that still catches the young woman's eye.

It's the front of Paul's car, its rather low-slung nose not far above the pavement, which reminds her of those minutes she'd spend watching for it when he came to her house, his parking maneuvers, and then the top of his head, the way he'd walk with his body bent a little forward, the noise he'd make in his throat, something between clearing and coughing, as if he wanted to put something back in its place, the speed with which he glided to her doorway.

In an attempt to save herself from a relapse, the young woman concentrates on a more recent memory: the morning when the man drove past her house and didn't turn his head toward it, as until then he hadn't been able to stop himself from doing since their breakup.

On that morning, then, Ema had stepped out of her house just in time to see him in profile, head straight and neck stiff. *Straight as a ruler*, she'd thought, and Paul, rigid as he was, had seemed to her ever so slightly ridiculous.

editor's note

John Christopher Cullen, the translator of this novel, passed away on April 15, 2021. We at Other Press were shaken by the news, and in the months that have since passed, our grief has not diminished. We had the good fortune of working with John for many years, on countless books. His uncanny sense of rhythm and nuance were hallmarks of his work, not to mention his warmth, humor, and intellect.

John submitted a complete translation of *Geography of an Adultery* but was not able to review the copyeditor's work or the galleys. Luckily he was always careful and meticulous from the get-go, and any editing or correcting that took place after submission was invariably light and minor. In other words, we are confident that this translation represents the text as John would have wanted it, though we will never know what finishing touches he might have added.

With great sadness, we say farewell to an irreplaceable translator and colleague, on his return to, in Proust's words, the place where artists and writers go before they are born.

AGNÈS RIVA lives in the suburbs of Paris, where she draws inspiration from its urban landscape. She is the author of the short story "New Life," which was published in the anniversary issue of the *New French Review*. Her debut novel, *Geography of an Adultery*, was short-listed for a Discovery Grant from the Prince Pierre de Monaco Foundation and was a finalist for the Prix Goncourt and Grand Prix RTL-Lire.

JOHN CULLEN (1942–2021) was the translator of many books from Spanish, French, German, and Italian, including Susanna Tamaro's *Follow Your Heart*, Philippe Claudel's *Brodeck*, Carla Guelfenbein's *In the Distance with You*, Juli Zeh's *Empty Hearts*, Patrick Modiano's *Villa Triste*, and Kamel Daoud's *The Meursault Investigation*.